THE REBIRTH OF NICODEMUS

RICK AKINS

En Route Books and Media, LLC
St. Louis, MO

ENROUTE
Make the time

En Route Books and Media, LLC
5705 Rhodes Avenue
St. Louis, MO 63109

Cover credit: TJ Burdick

Library of Congress Control Number:
2019948505

All scriptural quotes are from the New
International Version of the Bible.

Dedication

To my Parents, Ann and Dick Akins

CONTENTS

CONTENTS

Zero A.D.

"When King Herod heard this, he was greatly troubled, and all Jerusalem with him. Assembling all the chief priests and the scribes of the people, he inquired of them where the Messiah was to be born. They said to him, "In Bethlehem of Judea..."

Chapter 1

Wailing and Gnashing of Teeth

The older Pharisees and Scribes lied to our king.

"There is no prophesied leader," some said. "The Magi misread the glowing star in the sky." "We have only one king."

Herod's nameless adviser asked me, then, a proud and arrogant eighteen-year-old Scribe.

Me. Little more than a boy. Seven decades ago.

I had answered proudly, "I know where. The prophecy is in the book of Micah. He will be born south of the Holy City."

An hour later, as the crowds dispersed from the Temple after the Festival of Light, I marched among the lead element of the troops Herod sent out, seeking the child.

We swung sharply to the right and through a gate in the outer wall. The gate closed firmly behind us and we were enveloped in near blackness. A cool night wind blew up from the south, tickling the sweat upon my brow. The three mighty towers Herod erected

1

loomed to my right like sleeping giants, lit by shrouded lanterns as we passed.

We marched steadily, knocking pebbles off the road and kicking up a mist of dust. I fell back into the second cohort, outside the ranks and just barely upon the uneven edge of the roadway. Step-by-step, I allowed myself to fall back behind one rank after another. The lead elements receded into the night in front of me, lost except for the occasional cuss and growled command. I felt like a child seeking a place to hide within a suddenly grown-up world. In the Temple, even at my age, I received a certain level of respect. But among these ruffians....

"Where are we going?" I heard from behind.

I almost tripped over an unseen rock. I half-turned my head. A soldier had walked up behind me with a short torch in hand. Beside him walked Herod's adviser, whom I did not earlier notice.

I could not answer. I forced my feet forward, trying now to match the cadence of the troops.

"Tell me, wise one," the adviser growled. "You are the expert. Where is this new king?"

I shivered, though the night was not yet deeply cold. I glanced at the sky before us to the south, where the strange star had hung low over the hills for weeks on end. There was only the common host twinkling in the night sky now, broken up by a scattering of cloud.

We marched first toward the east, around the southern tip of Jerusalem's walls. We eased to the right and found footing on the main southern road. There was a slight and very welcomed descent. After a mile or two, we rose again. Not a steep climb by any means, but for those around me fully laden with armor, it was difficult. After another half-hour, the troops both before and behind me cursed each step. These were not the soldiers of Rome. These were the uneducated and drunkards who sold themselves into the service of our half-Jewish king.

I wondered at the presence of so many soldiers around me. Even if they wanted to find the 'new king' the visitors from the east had asked about, only a few soldiers were needed to bring the baby back for Herod to honor. And it would be much safer to do so by day, so why did we now march long after sunset?

I glanced often toward Herod's adviser, but the man marched on alone, his face set. Like most of us living in Jerusalem, he had little interest in the world outside the city. When you spend your entire life within the city of the king, or in my case with the King of Heaven in worship and study, why worry or think about the trivialities of the world? Despite the burning hopes in each of our breasts, most of us understood the time for a new Jewish empire was far in the future.

I turned my head, trying not to stumble as we marched. Many miles behind us now, my young eyes saw only a few twinkling lights at the main gates of Jerusalem. The celebrations had ended, so even the Temple area was dark except for the watch fires.

A new king, I thought. *A new king*.

I stopped. My heart beat hard in my chest.

The troop marched on. After a moment or two, Herod's adviser noticed me and moved toward me, both hands fisted by his sides.

"A king," I whispered to myself. "A new king."

I looked back to the south, straight along our path. There, who knows how far off in the dark, waited the town of Bethlehem. This was the town the men from the east would have come to had they properly understood the Scriptures.

Did our visitors find what they had sought? Did they see a baby only, or perhaps a child they thought was much more? They had not returned as Herod had commanded. Why? What did they know? What did they find in Bethlehem, the city toward which I was now leading Herod's troops? What did they suspect? The same idea now entering my naïve mind? That a new King would be a threat?

I stared into the dark toward Sahour. Our road would split not a quarter mile ahead of us, going either toward this town of legend or straight on to the hometown of David. The first section of troops had now paused at the fork in the road. There was still time. Sahour was a small village following the terrible fire set there three years earlier by the retreating Roman legion. There couldn't be more than a dozen homes. Perhaps we wouldn't even find a baby boy there. Then, perhaps, we could return to Jerusalem.

Herod's adviser came to my side and without comment swung

his arm and hit me across the ear. It was not painful, but it shook me instantly from my thoughts.

"The King's kindness is not as quick as his temper," he said. His face was but a foot from my own. It stank of stale alcohol. His cratered face came clear, highlighted in gold as several soldiers gathered with additional torches. "His reward for your information is easily lost. I am in no mood to march around this night in circles. If you do not tell me now, I will have the man right behind you cut your guts out and paint the road red with your blood. The birds and dogs will have you devoured by morning before anyone even knows you are gone."

"Where," he said slowly, "is...the...new....king?"

"There is no king," I said. "We read only of a prophet..."

The man across from me glanced up over my right shoulder. I squeezed my back against the tip of the sword I pictured being thrust toward me. Instead, another fist punched me in the back of the head. I was pushed forward. The adviser's hands shot up into my shoulders to catch and steady me.

"I have more hungry Jews in my employment than you," he said. "I know exactly what we are searching for, and I am confident I know where to find it. But I have to know for sure."

He grabbed my hair above my ear and pulled me close.

"Our King does not need to know of your hesitation. He would not appreciate your wasting our time. But I need to know now. Confirm this for me. Where is this newborn king?"

I looked over the man's shoulder toward the south. Behind me, it seemed all the eyes of my people and my God were staring at me from the direction of the Temple.

Slowly, I raised my arm, pointing in between Sahour to the right and Bethlehem ahead and slightly to the left. I forced my arm in that direction. My breath shuddered in my chest.

When my arm was even with his shoulder, the adviser turned and looked down the length of my arm in the direction of my pointing finger.

My hand stood out, gold and trembling before a background of black. Far beyond, still a mile or more away, stood the lit gate of silent Bethlehem.

"Bethlehem," I croaked. "He is to be born there."

The adviser pushed my arm down. He nodded to the soldier to my left. The man thrust the hilt of his sword into my side, at the base of my ribs. Breath shot through my lips and I crumbled onto my knees.

Above me, I heard the adviser cry in a loud voice, "There! Straight ahead."

There was a mixture of angry shouts and sour laughter from the troops. The adviser grabbed a torch from one of his assistants and marched quickly up the side of the roadway to the front of the guard.

"Find this king!"

A few of the soldiers held their daggers aloft and hooted. Others snarled like fell dogs. Their yells were swallowed by the wastelands to either side. Soon, all I could hear was the double-time stamping of booted feet moving away from me southward along the road. I picked up the edges of my robes and hustled behind the last row of soldiers, slowly falling into deeper and deeper darkness as Herod's soldiers left me behind. Within minutes, I was all alone upon the road.

All alone, when the first screams rolled over the plain like the call of demons circling in the night. Young human yelps cut short as if a pack of feral dogs was being put down. Then the screams. The screams!

I collapsed upon a large boulder just off the side of the road, my hands trembling upon my knees. A gathering of torch light rose above the short walls of Bethlehem, rushing wildly back and forth. The hoarse shouts of soldiers rose for a few minutes only, then they too passed into silence, leaving only the wailing cries of old women.

Two hours after they left me behind, the first of Herod's men came back, marching under half-used, faintly glowing torches, kicking stones and dust before them. They stared at me as they passed. Some with pity, most with anger, I suppose, or disgust. There had been no glory for them that night. Just slaughter. And slaughter is tiring work. Bitter work. And who better to be angry at than the betrayer?

I sat alone, unable to flee, feeling the sticky rain of the soldiers' spit, the sting of the rocks they kicked at me or threw.

The road was again empty as the sun rose slowly to my left. By now, the dust had settled over the road. I heard far off to the north, toward Jerusalem, sounds of people making their way to investigate the tumult of the night before. I stood, my legs stiff, and stumbled back to the road. I pulled the top of my cloak over my head to shield my face and shuffled toward Bethlehem. I reached the shattered gate in less than half an hour, even though I slowed as I approached.

There was only death. Silence and death. Worse than any scene of battle I would ever experience. Much worse. There was no smoke. No fire. None of the back and forth insanity of battle. No victors. Just victims.

The sun-lit sky was unmerciful. Horribly, perfectly clear, making matters all the worse. Bethlehem's gate had been crushed in from the middle, the only visible mark of destruction from outside the town. A woman stood in the gateway, bloodied and dazed. She saw my Pharisaic dress and held her arms up to the heavens, then stumbled out toward me.

"You've come!" she screamed. "Praise the Lord you've come. But it's too late. It is too late!"

She rushed at me and I pulled back, suddenly terrified.

What has happened? I thought. But I knew, didn't I? Of course I did, I knew what was going to happen as I marched from the City with Herod's men, all too well. I knew when I raised my hand toward this town of David what would happen here.

I knew.

The woman grabbed me and pulled me with all her might through the city gate. There, in bright morning colors, lay a small body covered in drying scarlet. A boy only, his child's face staring into the sky. I could see the dark muddy blue of his young eyes. Could he have been any older than a toddler?

I shook off the woman's claws and moved to another child, moving my body to shield his open eyes from the rising sun. Beside this boy, another, face down, his right arm severed and laying small and stubby a few paces away. This child was partially covered by the body of his father. The man's heel prints displayed where he had

6

been dragged through the dusty ground all the way back to a small hut near the center of the town. I imagined him holding his child with such force they could not be separated by Herod's men until this very spot.

One by one, the surviving townspeople came out, girls and older boys in tow. They came directly at me, seeing in me a savior from the Temple. A savior instead of a coward and a scoundrel.

All around me was carnage. Death. Even those I watched sobbing had long since cried themselves into tearless whispers.

All this, so as to end the King of the Jews before he could threaten the king in Jerusalem. All this, to do away with a baby who, I would later learn, had already been brought by his parents to the Temple for consecration. I knew this would be their way, for that is the way for all first-born Jewish boys. They would not have been here. Why didn't I think of this the evening before?

All this death, for nothing. Dozens of children murdered. Because I had betrayed them.

69 A.D.

Chapter 2

Well Met

"You are John?"

The dark figure stood erect within my doorway. I squinted against the daylight streaming in from the lane outside my home. I seldom had visitors, unannounced. I thought at that moment of indecision that at my age, there is really neither the time nor the need to fear.

"Yes, I am John," the man said.

His accent still betrayed Galilean roots but there was more than a hint of foreignness. He looked into my home's outer room, taking in my remaining possessions.

What are you possibly doing here? I thought. *And why now of all times?*

I raised my hand in greeting. John closed the door and a quiet dimness returned to my home. He walked toward me. He was a large man, with hair just graying around the temples. His eyes were surrounded by the deep creases of all sunbaked fishermen. He stopped a pace before me, hands grasped before his waist. His eyes looked at me steadily, patiently.

"My granddaughter said she heard you had returned," I told John. "Of course, we also all hear stories about the Romans marching back toward the Holy City, so I doubted you were here. They hate your people almost as much as mine."

I looked at Anna, standing next to me, and gently touched her forearm. My daughter nodded her head slightly at our guest and retired to the kitchen. She did not particularly like John's people, and certainly not since my granddaughter began to talk about their ways.

I motioned for him to sit beside me and his shadowed face lit up before the candles burning upon my table.

"*The* John?" I grinned. "You are such a man now. So different than the last time we met."

He chuckled. It was not the polite laugh I have heard throughout my life. No, this was the belly laugh containing a joy I couldn't help but join with a smile.

"How old were you back then?"

"I am surprised you remember," John said. "I was perhaps eighteen."

He leaned his walking stick against the post to his right. He reached down and placed his hand upon my own. I fought the sudden urge to pull back, yet something coaxed me to hold still.

"What can I do for you?" I asked.

Surely, I thought, he had come to gain my support, to speak up for him and his people before the Sanhedrin. My old colleagues had been emboldened against John's people since they forced the Romans from the Holy City a couple of years ago.

"Do you actually remember that night?" he asked. His eyes were suddenly stern. His tone grew anxious.

I paused and stared at the man, now in his early fifties, three decades younger than me.

"What?"

He leaned forward.

"The night you came to him. I was in awe of you. The leader of our people. *The* Nicodemus," he teased. "I tried to sear each word of your discussion with him into my mind. But so much has happened since. I need to get everything right."

"Get what right?"

John reached under his tunic and pulled out a small scrap of papyrus. Maybe three inches to a side. He placed it flat upon the table and pushed it toward me. I waited for a few moments, listening to my neighbors pass outside my window. For a moment I felt as if my life, what little was left of it, would change forever if I touched and read that paper. Even then, I knew.

"What is that?"

"A few words only. I don't dare move about with more," John said. "I am growing old and I have seen so many of my friends murdered these past few years. Word has also recently come from Rome. Terrible tidings. Terrible. I will soon be gone, if that is the will of God. But before then, I must tell the story."

"Yes," I said. "I think that is wise. Smart also that you only carry a small piece, I presume, of what you've written. Something easily burned, if needed."

John pressed his lips together. The last I saw him up close, he still had the bare face of a boy. Now, he was fully bearded.

"What did he say?" he asked.

My fingers touched the paper, trembling slightly as I pulled the edge toward me. I held it before my face, tilting it toward the daylight coming through the window behind me. I read slowly, carefully. As I did, that night so long ago became clear in my mind. I remembered that face. The face of Jesus in the firelight. I was a bit younger then than John was as I saw him this day. Almost forty years ago.

After a second reading of what was no more than three dozen words, I placed the writing facedown and slid it back toward my visitor.

"You write well, my lad, for a fisherman." I smiled at the thought of calling him a lad, and he smiled back. "But from what I hear you are now quite learned, and in charge of a great many things." I paused. "You have remembered correctly concerning the part you wrote."

John let out a trembling breath and reached for his writing.

I leaned back, stretching my sore shoulders. I felt suddenly tired. This man's people had caused me many headaches - and more - for almost forty years. And yet, at an age when I thought I would simply one day fail to wake, here sat John. Silence filled my home as we both sensed this was the last moment I could politely ask him to leave, and leave me be.

John returned the papyrus under his cloak. He placed his hands in his lap and waited quietly.

"Except for one thing," I offered.

John leaned forward until both elbows rested on his knees. He looked up at me, deep creases forming across his brow. "What part?"

I grabbed the small wooden cup set next to me and took a sip, moving the cool water around my mouth. I swallowed, then took a deep breath and held it fast.

The part, I thought, *that threatens the entire faith of our people*.

"He told me that night," I exhaled slowly, "and I do remember what he said exactly because he repeated it. He could tell I did not fully under...."

"What did he say?" John interrupted. "That you needed to be born again?"

I chuckled but stopped short just as I sensed my laugh would again turn into a cough.

"No. Look at me. I wish I could be born again. And I knew what he meant by that, we are to be spiritually born again, to wash away all our sins and break down all that separates us from the Lord. How often in Scripture did the Lord call our people to repent? No, your teacher and I had our little verbal parry about that, but I understood his meaning well enough."

I leaned my head back, closed my eyes, and thought of that moment long ago, returning to the dark night. "No, what confused me....what confuses me still, was when he said to me, 'The Spirit goes where it wills.'"

John said nothing. I lingered over those long-ago spoken words. After a moment, I lowered my head, opening my tired eyes to stare at my dirt floor.

"What did he mean by that?" I asked.

"You have heard," he said.

"I have heard much."

"And you still do not know?"

"I do not," I said. But, perhaps I did.

"Well," John said, "will you come with me? I have much to show you."

I looked quickly toward the kitchen, then down to the table-top propping up my left forearm.

"I am old," I said. "Though I may be forgotten by the world, I have my Anna and my granddaughter here to protect. And I will soon be going to the Lord."

"Yes." John smiled behind his graying beard. I stared at him. "You may indeed. But you still have much to tell me. And I have much to show you."

I blew a breath out between my teeth. My hands clenched in my lap. I slowly shook my head. "No."

The man across from me slapped his thighs with his hands and stood quickly. He nodded with deep respect.

"Then, may I return later, Rabbi Nicodemus?" He made his way to the door. "I need you. We all need you. I need to hear the whole story about when you first met the Lord. I must figure out what to write. And perhaps I can provide an answer to what confused you so much that night."

I smiled and shrugged.

"You are certainly welcome back. Maybe you can tell me something I don't know. I might also tell you about my first meeting with Jesus of Nazareth. It was not what you think. It was not *when* you think."

Chapter 3

Waking and Dying

I woke the next morning clutching my pillow. Awakened by John's visit, the images of those little faces, murdered almost seventy years ago, floated lifeless in my thoughts. My bedclothes were sticky with hot sweat.

Over the course of the next hour, I heard Anna come to the door a few times, twice tapping softly and calling my name.

I could not face myself. How could I possibly face her?

Eventually her patience ran out, or her fear grew enough for her to firmly knock at my door.

"Father," she asked, "are you okay? It's a pretty day out, perhaps we should take a walk? Do you feel up to going to the Temple?"

I rolled away from my daughter's voice and stared at the wall. My eyes teared before the crack of light seeping past the edges of my shutter. I sighed, my lungs burning close to the edge of a cough.

The Temple, I thought. I shook my head as my hands clenched into fists around my pillow. I closed my eyes and wished with all my heart that my daughter would leave.

Instead, she creaked open the door and came to my bedside. She sat down softly next to me. Her fingers ran through my sparse hair and she gently rubbed my shoulder and neck.

"Are you in pain?" she asked. "It is that John, isn't it? I knew he would do you no good. I will send him away next time."

I closed my eyes and shook my head. I took a shuddering breath and opened my mouth to speak. Nothing but a rough sigh came out. I forced my eyes open, letting the light scare away the images of those young babies so long ago. To put away once again my thoughts

15

of their parents' agony during that bloody morning of my treachery.

"I am an old man," I said. "I served my Lord and his Temple all these years. I tried to help many people…"

"Yes," my daughter said firmly. She pushed herself off the bed and stood over me. "Yes, you are a wonderful man, father."

"So why can't I just die in peace?" I groaned. I wiped my eyes against my pillow. The cloth smelled sour. "Haven't I earned at least that much?"

I held my breath, listening intently, hoping my daughter would return to the kitchen and leave me in peace. But I knew she would not.

Lord, I prayed. *You gave me the last several years to take care of her after Matthias was killed. She's old enough to be a grandmother. How can she take care of herself? Look at me now! How can I take care of her much longer?*

Anna stepped back and forth. She took a breath and exhaled loudly, then another breath as if she was going to speak. Finally, she walked away. She paused at the door and I could picture her standing as she often did, arm resting against the door frame, face leaned toward the floor. I ground my teeth, waiting breathlessly for her next words of encouragement. I just could not take any more encouragement from her.

Instead, I heard someone else enter the room.

"Grandfather?"

Miriam….

She walked to me and gently touched my cheek with soft fingers.

"Grandfather," she said again, "can I ask a favor?"

I sensed her look over her shoulder toward her mother. For a moment, I felt a trace of anger at Anna, for this was her oft repeated ploy to get me moving in the more difficult mornings.

I rolled over and Miriam stood. With all my might, I pushed my legs out over the edge of the bed and Miriam helped me into a sitting position. That action, along with the cool morning air gripping my body, shocked away the horrible images of my pre-dawn dreams.

I looked into my granddaughter's face and smiled the best I could. Her eyes were dark but lively, her raven black hair fell long over her shoulders. She wore an outer tunic of pale blue, her apron already cinched into her belt. I reached for her hand, feeling the golden bracelet I had given her years before. I suddenly thought of her as a young child, back when I could afford the gold dust Anna would sprinkle into Miriam's hair to make it sparkle.

"Grandfather," Miriam said. She cradled both of my hands in hers. They were warm.

"You actually do have a favor to ask?"

"Yes, grandfather," she said, now stooping to take a knee before me.

"Abram needs to attend to the Temple tonight. But I was wondering if he could join us for our noon meal? I believe he wants to discuss something with you after we finish."

Abram, I thought with a smile. They had been courting for many months now. Finally, he came to speak to me. I glanced at Anna, who smiled broadly near the door.

"Of course, he can speak with me," I said. "And share our meal, if it is alright with your mother."

I squeezed Miriam's fingers and she turned to rush from my room. She paused for only a moment at the door and gave her mother an excited kiss on the cheek. Anna tried to kiss her in return, but Miriam was already gone, leaving us nothing but the echo of an excited giggle.

Anna turned to me, her dark eyes glistening in the morning light.

"He's a good man," she said. "I know you fear for Miriam, that she will suffer again as she did when she was widowed. But she is lonely, and he is a good man."

I shivered.

"Anna," I asked, "Could you please get your old father something warm to wear?"

She pressed her lips together and nodded, knowing that for at least one more morning she had successfully brought me into the world. That seemed to be enough. But as I waited for her to come back with my shawl, I looked up to the ceiling, to the Lord I long served. To the Lord I could no longer feel present around me. The Lord who refused to take me home. The Almighty who had left me, alone, to struggle with my guilt.

Anna returned and wrapped a blanket around my shoulders.

"And what about John?" I asked Anna. "I thought I heard a strange voice in the house when I first woke. Did John come here this morning?"

"He was here. I told him you had been awake much of the night and I would not know when you would be ready to see him. He said he'd wait outside. I peeked through the door a couple of times; he is sitting in the doorway across the lane. Then, when Miriam came back home a little while ago, she said she spoke with him and they walked up and down the lane a few times."

For the briefest moment, I pictured young Miriam walking along the mid-morning streets with John. She would have gone willingly with him, of course. Despite all I had taught her about God and our people's faith, there was still something about the stories concerning the Nazarene that excited her. I never told her about my times with that man, literally from his birth to his death. Since we repulsed the Romans from the Holy City a few years ago, what stories were still told about Jesus were spoken of in whispers. And after Abram, a Temple guardsman, began to court my granddaughter, I thought all would finally be well. Another task achieved. She and her children would remain solidly among our people.

Anna brought me water and a middle section of crustless bread by the time I reclined at our table. She made bread fresh each morning, but even fresh crust hurt my mouth. It was already close to noon, so she also laid next to me a small bowl of crushed dates. Bless her, she always removed the tough skin and mashed up the inner pulp to give me a sweet something to spread across my bread. This morning, she also left a small mound of chopped olives upon my plate.

"When Miriam told me Abram asked if he could speak with you," Anna said, "I wanted to wake you earlier, but I heard you moan last night."

"I will be fine. I would ask why Abram is coming to see me, but her excitement seems answer enough."

I placed several chopped olive pieces in my mouth and carefully squeezed the meat with my tongue. I rubbed my eyes, steadying myself as I sat. My body began to respond to the food now. The uneasy thoughts of the previous night receded.

There was a light knock. Anna sprang up, then slowly pulled smooth her clothing and walked purposefully to the door.

"Abram!" she said. Miriam moved in her room behind me but she did not come out.

"Good morning," Abram said. He smiled broadly at my daughter and quickly placed his short sword and shield on the floor just inside the doorway.

"Please come sit," Anna said.

Abram stepped past her tentatively. As his eyes adjusted to the shadows within our home, he saw me and stopped.

"Rabbi Nicodemus," he sputtered.

"Are you surprised to see me?" I teased. "Did you not ask to lunch with me?"

"No," he said. "I mean, yes. I mean...."

He looked at Anna, his mouth falling into a frown.

"I am afraid I cannot enjoy your meal after all."

Miriam opened her door and rushed into the room.

"What? Why not?"

Abram's lips parted behind his short beard. He held his hands out to Miriam, then looked at me and brought them back to his sides.

"I apologize. There are many rumors about the Romans entering their new camp to the north. Some are worried they are far too close to the East Road. Thousands of pilgrims will soon pass over that road, coming to the Temple for Passover. I have been called in for instructions, I must go to the Temple right away."

Anna covered her mouth with both hands, looking wide-eyed at the young couple.

"I am sure there will be no problem," Abram said. "We're just being careful. You know how things can get out of hand with so many soldiers and people moving about."

"Well then," I said. I pushed myself up and took my walking staff from the edge of the table. I stepped slowly toward Abram. Miriam saw my smile and, covering her own face with her hand, stepped back from her friend.

"Since time is short, Abram, please tell me what you wanted to discuss."

Abram looked down to the floor and scraped his boot against the dirt. He glanced at Anna, then Miriam. Since neither seemed ready to leave us in privacy, he breathed deep and looked back at me.

"Rabbi," he said. "You know my father was killed some years ago, he was a good and faithful man, always your friend and a friend of the Temple."

"Yes," I said. "He was a man of great integrity and strength."

"Well," he said. "He was also smart and gathered some wealth for us. Unfortunately, I am not so smart, though I hope to prove to have learned at least his integrity. I let others take from my family these past few years. They have left me with little. Far too little to offer your beloved Miriam."

Miriam reached out to him, tears in her eyes.

"And," he continued, "Miriam's father, your son-in-law, was killed by the Romans, just a few years ago. Your Anna's husband, and Miriam's. The same night, both by the hands of the Romans. I knew them both, and they were good men. I could hope only to...."

"You are a good man yourself, Abram," Anna said.

Abram looked at her and his shoulders slumped forward. He gripped his hands before his chest, unable to look up at me.

"My daughter is right," I reassured him. "You are a loyal, honest man."

Abram sighed heavily. He nodded solemnly.

"Miriam," he said, "has no father for me to ask, and I have no father to ask. So, I ask you, good rabbi, may I have Miriam as my wife, though I have nothing but myself and my empty home to offer her."

My mind brought forth the memory of Anna's husband asking similar permission. I had great means then, of course, and yet I looked and waited, inspected the man and asked him again and again what he was offering my daughter.

Now...I have seen two widows made the same night within my family. Perhaps I could ask nothing more than that this good and strong man love by granddaughter and live an honorable life.

"Of course, my son," I said. "Of course, you both have my blessing."

How long had Abram been in my home? Five minutes, perhaps. And yet, I was already exhausted. It didn't help, of course, that the two women in my life didn't stop talking for the next hour, almost forgetting our noon meal altogether. Miriam left after eating a few bites, practically skipping out the door on her way back to her friends at the market.

Tired as I found myself, I could not have been happier. Miriam would live with Abram on this eastern side of the Temple, in his family home just a few lanes away. Abram was a man of the faith, born and raised by a dedicated Pharisee who worked and studied with me for decades. The ruin that fell upon his family after his father's murder was painful to watch, but in some ways, it seemed to have made Abram all the stronger and more loyal.

Plus, I thought with a smile, at least we could soon drink the best of the wine I had saved from our last vineyard yield.

My smile faded away. The sudden thought of my vineyards brought sadness, not from having sold them in recent years, but because of Herod. The king and his son had been some of my best customers through the years. Customers, I knew, who came my way due to the mistake I made on the road to Bethlehem those many decades ago. Patrons sent to me by a thankful King.

Anna brought me a wooden cup of a wine she must also have been saving in some hidden cabinet. We drank in silence, as content as we had been in a long time. Outside our little home, the rumors of Romans, the increasing anxiety over the coming Passover. Here, for a moment, peace. Anna closed her eyes several times, muttering a prayer of thanks. I closed my eyes with her, covering her hand with my own. Finally, she stood and excused herself to her room. She laid down and I heard a few soft sobs coming through her closed door.

I nibbled at a scrap of dark bread for a long while. There then came a light knock on the outer door.

"Rabbi?" I heard. The voice was John's.

I turned toward Anna's door, about to call her to attend to our visitor. Instead, I rocked myself forward, stood and walked unsteadily to grip the door handle, still cool and solid in the early afternoon.

The sunlight outside was brilliant, painting everything bright white and yellow. The smell of camel dung, fresh from the newly arrived caravans upon the East Road, came with the breeze blowing down from the north. The tinkling laughter of a group of young children echoed down our small lane from the right. I edged my way across the street, careful not to be trampled either by the young or a passing camel. I forgot my walking stick at my table and wobbled a bit as I walked.

John had moved away from our home after he knocked and sat in the doorway across the street. His head tilted against the frame, his eyes half-closed. But he heard my door open and was already beginning to get up. He reached out and grabbed my arm to steady me.

"Rabbi," he said with a bow of his head.

I turned to the left, for the lane dipped in that direction for a few dozen strides, before rising again toward the Temple wall. I motioned in that direction and walked forward slowly, moving away from my home. John joined me.

"Why?" I asked.

"Rabbi?"

"Why have you come back?"

I expected his hand to grip my arm tighter. Instead, he walked on, staring up at the massive walls before us.

We rounded the next corner, now heading south beneath the warm sun. I hadn't planned it, but perhaps we would wind around the rows of homes in this area and circle back to my home.

"I told you the other day," John started.

"Yes!" I interrupted, a bit more sharply than I had planned. "I understand. You have come to me, a leader of the Jewish people, a Pharisee, and you expect me to tell you some mysterious things about your Jesus so you can turn other Jews away from our faith."

"Rabbi Nicodemus," John said, releasing my upper arm. He stopped. "I have not meant to offend. I have not come here to pull you or your family or anyone else from the faith of our fathers. I too am a Jew. I also grew up to expect and desire and hope for the

Messiah. We believe he has come. But I respect you and I am not here to do anything to hurt the Chosen People of the Lord."

He turned to me and stared into my eyes.

"The truth is, I am now a leader of the people who follow in our ways. In fact, I am the last of the leaders who actually were there."

He swept his hand past the Temple and toward the Mount of Olives to the south.

"Actually present. With him. Everyone now wants me to write his story. But I don't know what to say. I really don't know how to write. I pray for the guidance of the Spirit every day. All I know is that I must write. And, I must get everything correct."

I stared at him and saw no deception in his eyes.

"But why me?" I asked.

"Because you alone know about things you've done with my Lord. You alone came to him with your questions that night, and you alone seemed willing to consider him. I am the only one left, and in a way, so are you."

I looked at my feet. My toes were twisted angrily beneath a light coating of dust. I tipped my head back to the blue sky above.

"So, you came to me now because you know that I am an old man only wanting to die and go to God?"

John smiled and grabbed both my hands in his. They were strong, rough and warm.

"No, good teacher!" he said. "You may live long still. I am not worried about you dying with your stories untold."

He paused and shook his head. He took a deep, trembling breath.

"No, I came here when I heard about Paul. My brother James was murdered twenty years ago. Stephen was stoned, as you know. All the others. Murdered. All of them. Last of them, Paul. And that leaves only me, the final witness. How much longer do you think I have? I came here because I know this is my last chance. You may not die soon, my father, but my time is limited."

We resumed our walk. We turned onto a lane and slowly climbed. Thankfully, our side of the lane rested in the shade. Still, I began to sweat as we made it to the top and turned left for a third time on our trek.

"I have to confess," John said. He moved very close to me and began in a whisper. "There is more. I must leave in three weeks, when Passover ends. In fact, I fear perhaps we all must leave."

I stopped short and felt my knees almost buckle. John held me up and led me to the side of the lane to sit within a doorway. I shook him off and stood strong again.

"What do you mean?"

John looked to his left and right. The lane was mostly empty. He gently indicated I should sit.

"You asked why I came now. It is not for myself alone, or for my people, that I am concerned. I heard the report of Paul's death from a centurion who has come to the faith. A man I would trust with my very life. He brought me the sad news just one month ago. He was also the one who gave me the sad details of Peter's gruesome crucifixion last year. The Romans in the capital slaughter my people. But the empire has been in chaos, almost in a civil war from what we understand in Ephesus."

"Yes, I have heard rumors of this," I said.

"The Roman distractions have protected all of us," John said. "And the Lord in heaven, of course. But now my centurion friend, and others, bring news that Rome is settling down behind a single emperor. Their conflicts are ended."

This I had not heard. Even with the Romans reestablishing a garrison just north of my home, I had heard little. I wondered if those leading our people, and overseeing the Temple, had heard more.

"You did not know this? Yes. All true. Stability in Rome is not good news. Now we hear the word has gone forth. Even as far as Ephesus. Issues, and insults, that had been left alone are now going to be addressed. The threats Rome sees here and elsewhere are going to be answered."

I felt the blood leave my face. I could not breathe. I knew exactly what John meant. However, until I heard him say these words aloud my mind would not allow for the possibility.

"I don't know anything for sure," he said, "except the Romans are on the move. Their ships passed through Ephesus. Their armies march in this direction. Your people expelled them from Jerusalem three years ago. It seems this challenge will now be answered. And I have to believe they will do more than answer. They come here to make a point. And the best time to make the point against us, and against our God...."

I looked at John, horrified.

"Will be at Passover."

Chapter 4

Old Friends

She was afraid.

I remember well the night Miriam's husband went out with the others. The entire city was aroused. It seemed there was a chance to free ourselves from the Romans. God was moving among us.

But I knew better.

Well, I didn't know better, actually, for the following morning we did find that the Romans had abandoned Jerusalem. Gone. Praise the Lord above!

But, yes, I knew better. There was nothing to be excited about. Not that night and the day that followed. For many died in the struggle.

Miriam had been first in line with a hug and a kiss for her husband-rebel. I watched her proudly hand a sword to Zecheri, her smile gleaming in the torch light. The sight broke my heart.

Today, three years later, she has learned. There was nothing immediately desperate with Abram's call to the Temple. The Romans were setting up camp, sure, but there were few of them. Had it not been for John's warning about Passover, I am not sure my thoughts would have been the least troubled.

But, Miriam knew better. She brooded deeper and deeper after Abram left for his duties.

After our lunch, I waited for the sun to descend behind the walls of the Temple and then cut Miriam's list of chores short. I grabbed her cold hand and told her that her grandfather needed a walk in

27

the remaining warmth of the day. She kissed me on the cheek and gladly led the way.

About an hour passed, interrupted by several long pauses as I rested. We moved off the dirt and cobbled paths and into the gardens and wastelands beyond. When I first mentioned Abram, her grip on my hand turned almost painful. But, soon, I was discussing what I and Anna might be able to provide them as they set up their new home. Her laughter resurrected and brought out the colors of the wildflowers around the path we walked. My soul sang, to be able to bring such joy and promise for her as I had for her mother thirty years earlier!

We edged along again, my thoughts lost along paths of remembrances as I looked east toward my old vineyards. I did not notice that we turned ever to our left, ever toward the north. My lungs eventually noticed the gradual uphill and I needed to stop once again to rest to catch my breath. I held a small sapling tree and lowered myself onto an oblong boulder, shuffling my back side to find a moment of comfort.

"Who is that, grandfather?" Miriam asked.

I looked up. Her smooth face was lit pink now by the setting sun. She shaded her eyes with her left hand and pointed, cautiously, with her right, which she held low near her midsection.

I turned and blinked a few times to focus. I had not realized we had come so close to the East Road. It would have been jammed with people and livestock hours earlier, but it was now nearly empty. I saw why. There, standing upon it, were three Roman soldiers.

Two soldiers stood on either side and just behind the other. It was hard to make out the third's face, but he looked familiar to me for some reason.

"Miriam," I said. "Can you please....Miriam, look at me."

My granddaughter pulled her eyes from the Romans. She looked down at me, eyes wide in alarm.

"Miriam. Do not worry. No Roman soldier would ever start a fight with only two of their comrades nearby. These three are only looking. They are just making their presence known, standing on this road where so many of our people will soon pass. But I do not want them to know you by sight. There is no need for that. And...."

Miriam stepped toward me quickly and grabbed my arm roughly. I pulled myself free.

"Miriam! Listen to me. We are within sight of the Temple wall. For all we know, Abram might be up there right now looking down at you. What happens if he sees you here, so close to the Romans? He will rush out here on his own and he's likely to be killed. You know that."

Miriam's arms fell to her sides. She looked up toward the Temple wall, then moved to hide herself behind the sapling.

"I will not leave you here alone," she demanded.

"I understand. But I believe I might know the Roman up there on the road, the one in the middle. I must take advantage of this chance to talk to him. Perhaps I can get him to tell me why their troops have returned. You know the fools in the Temple will not bother to talk to these soldiers until it is too late.

"Please," I asked, "help me up."

A few minutes later, I stood at the bottom edge of the East Road. The flat paved surface, one of the few good things the Romans had left behind, was roughly even with my head, standing atop a sloping dirt shoulder. I leaned on my walking stick, desperate for air but unwilling to show my full eighty-seven years.

As I approached, the Roman commander told his guards to wait behind him, and he picked his way down the hillside of loose stone until he stood just a few strides away. His scarlet cloak fluttered in the wind behind him. He held his helmet under his left arm, pressed against his side.

Aetius. Once the commander of the Roman garrison in the Holy City. He and I had long conversed about the happenings of my people and various ways to keep peace within Jerusalem. We often met here in this area, for I would not and could not enter his station. When the Zealots began their efforts some ten years earlier, our discussions brought no aide to either side and he eventually cut off communication. Then, perhaps five years ago, the Emperor had replaced him with a commander, I suppose, who was thought more capable of dealing with a brewing rebellion.

Aetius' hair was roughly cut and graying. His skin hung loose from his jaw. A bandage covered an empty right eye-socket.

"I thought it was you," I said.

"You are old," he replied.

I began to laugh, then felt the smile leave my face. For all the banter of acquaintances we once shared, there was no humor now in his words. I realized immediately—his words were merely a statement of cold fact.

I gripped my walking stick and stood as tall as I could.

"And you are blind."

Perhaps there appeared a momentary grin then at the edge of his mouth. Perhaps not. He looked over my head toward the homes far behind me – my village – and sighed.

"This," he said, pointing to his lost eye, "was my gift to celebrate your people's rebellion."

"But...but you were no longer the commander here."

"No," he said. His voice was dry and rough. "No, I wasn't. But what does that matter?"

"I am sorry."

"Aren't we all."

We stood for a moment in silence. I then heard the clash of arms from behind the road, Romans soldiers keeping up their skills in the cool of the late afternoon. I noticed that my old acquaintance's uniform was no longer that of a Legatus, but a Praefectus. Demoted to one who merely sets up camps.

"I didn't know for sure," Aetius said, "if you were still alive. I heard rumors. About you and your daughter and your granddaughter."

"Yes," I said, "they are fine."

"Good. Your daughter was never exactly nice to me, but always respectful. Hate did not fill her eyes as it did so many others."

"She is a fine woman."

"Fine. Yes. You know, if not for your Jewish pride, we could have probably been friends, you and me. Me and them. It happens elsewhere where our legionary flags wave."

He slapped his hand against his helmet and took a deep breath.

"But not here. No, never here. I always received you and spoke to you as a man. And then, after I was called away, your daughter's husband and your granddaughter's husband – well, they both took up arms. They joined the rebellion against my Emperor. And I am rewarded with this."

He pulled his short dagger from his scabbard and pointed the tip toward his eye. I noticed his guards step toward the near edge of the road, not that Aetius needed any protection from me.

But I wasn't worried about myself at that moment.

"My girls did you no harm," I said. "You were not even here. And, both are now widows, so I think they suffered every bit as much as you."

Aetius looked up toward his men and waved them back.

"Perhaps. Well, now that we have met, my old friend, I will treat you as a friend, though I know you could never truly do the same."

He took a couple of steps toward me and lowered his voice.

"My old Nicodemus. Take my advice. Leave. Take your women and leave this place. Today."

I backed away, almost losing my footing.

"Leave the Holy City?"

"I cannot protect you. I will not even try."

I pointed to the Temple with my walking stick.

"This is my home. The home of God. I cannot leave. I will not even try."

Aetius nodded. He lifted his helmet and pulled it over his head, carefully passing over his missing eye.

"I shall never see you again, my rabbi," Aetius said, "Titus is coming. And with him, hell itself. I hope for your sake your God can protect you against it."

Aetius turned and marched away, his muddied scarlet cloak fluttering behind.

I turned my eyes away from him and toward the Temple. My arm shook as I let down my walking stick. The looming walls which always seems so massive, the very footstool of the almighty God, suddenly felt hollow.

My eyes drifted to the left, down toward the rooftops that surrounded our home. What was I to do? What could my people possibly do?

Chapter 5

Good Teacher

The following morning, I sat near the window looking into my home's small courtyard, letting the smell of life fill me.

"Are you tired?" John asked. "Do you want me to come back?"

I took a deep breath and stretched my shoulders.

"No, no, my son. I was just thinking. Actually, thinking quite a bit about what we discussed yesterday. My thoughts and worries have tired me. Your concerns about the Romans and Passover was not something I had considered. But after my run in with an old friend yesterday...."

He looked at me with sadness. I looked back, grinned and winked.

"Yes, I am sure. Please stay. Sometimes at my age, thoughts plague you and you cannot shake them. I do not have either a productive life or the interests of your young life to distract my mind. Perhaps you can help. You told me you are struggling to write. You asked about the night I first met Jesus."

"Yes."

John nodded curtly, looking at me with a quizzical grin.

Miriam entered from the kitchen behind me. She placed one wooden cup before each of us. She then fussed about me, doing nothing of actual value but looking at me sideways from several angles to make sure I was feeling alright.

"My meeting Jesus is quite a story. Three stories in one, I suppose. Three times where our paths met, me and your Nazarene.

One was not a happy occasion at all. Probably not fit for what you want to write, but maybe something you need to know nonetheless."

We sat quietly for a few moments. I did not yet feel ready to tell John of the night I nearly ended the infant's life.

Miriam sat upon the edge of a cushion in the corner of the room. She had far too much interest in the people of John, but I let her stay. She pretended to work then with some fabric she had brought with her, but I knew her sharp mind was focused upon our visitor. She wore a rough tan garment today, one of the many her late husband had saved up to give her once the Romans were beat and trade returned to the City. One of the many his money had purchased after his death.

"John," I said. "It might help me to know what information you are seeking, exactly. What are you trying to express in your scroll?"

"That I am so lonely," he said. A few moments passed in silence as if he had just told me everything. He lifted his water cup, his hand shaking slightly before his face, and took a small sip.

"No, of course not," he said. "Yes, I am lonely. I am the last to know a story that is almost impossible to talk about to someone who wasn't there and had not seen.

"I don't know what you remember following the crucifixion. I'm sure you heard rumors. There were once twelve of us, including the thief. The betrayer. Then, after Jesus went to the Father, dozens came to believe in him. Then hundreds, thousands. Can you imagine? Day after day for dozens of years now I have told the stories, and day after day complete strangers decide to change their lives because of Jesus. Here in Jerusalem. In Ephesus where I live. I've met many thousands more, from here to Rome itself.

"These thousands of souls now look to me as their leader. I understand their need, for only the twelve really knew him. I mean, we knew Jesus in the way children know their parents and their siblings. He told us everything. He showed us, well, he showed us things I cannot describe. Rabbi, he showed us the Father! I was there when everyone else abandoned him. Some of us were there during his time of anguish in the garden. We were there when he walked back through our locked door. I...I was there...."

His voice quaked and he took another drink. This time with

purpose.

"You were also with him on the hill," I said.

I remembered that very hour. I left the hill before Jesus died, but I well recall this man's young face as he stood watch beside the Nazarene's mother near the foot of the cross.

John lowered his cup to the table next to him, glanced at Miriam and then back to me.

"Yes," he said. "The most horrible moment of my life. Yet, even then I understood. Something kept me from despair, and something kept me from fear. Fear from you. From our Jewish leaders, I mean. But I didn't fear them, and I didn't fear the Romans as I waited for him to die."

"And yet now you do fear," I said.

"Not for me. I will certainly die like the others, I understand that, all too well. But I do not pause in the face of my death. I only fear for the others."

I nodded and looked through the window.

"Yes," I said, "there is much tension in Jerusalem. As you said, there are many Romans now in the valleys and fields outside the walls. We were told the emperor blames your people for the fire in Rome some years back. And my people also have killed many of your friends here in the Holy City. I'm not sure if I can help you with the other leaders in the Sanhedrin. I have not been to their meetings for some time now."

John shook his head.

"You don't understand," he said. "Peter has been killed. Paul has been killed. James. My poor brother, James! Those who follow the way of Jesus demand that I, as the last eyewitness, write his story. How can I possibly do that story justice? How can I even begin to choose what to say? I could fill up a dozen books with his life and still I wouldn't know if a single sentence would be worthy."

He paused.

"Haven't others already written?" I began, trying to lessen the pressure John felt.

"We heard of a scroll written by someone named Mark," Miriam said.

I glanced at her, shocked. She looked back into her lap.

"Yes," John said. "There is also a lengthy letter from the doctor, Luke. How can I possibly write as well as he did? And our brother Mark traveled with Peter. What can I add to what they have already said?"

"Well," I suggested. "Fill in what they did not write about. I don't know, write about what's happened since the others finished their stories. Certainly, much has changed."

I lifted my cup and wet my lips.

"Most of all," I said, "Pray and trust in the Spirit of God. If what you believe is true, the Spirit will guide you to write that truth."

I leaned toward John.

"I have often wondered, my son, how did Isaiah know what to write? Where did Ezekiel get such vivid images? When David and Solomon wrote, were they simply writing songs that touch our hearts? Or is there more to learn from their verses? I am sure the prophets must have trusted the Lord to help them write. What did it mean when they write, 'Thus says the Lord...'? Did the Lord speak to them as you and I are now speaking?

"Most of our Scripture came from men who didn't wait to hear the Lord through these," I touched my right ear. "God guided their hearts and minds through prayer and contemplation. Pray, my son, and trust."

John looked at Miriam and sighed heavily. He stood with a smile, turned toward the door, but then turned and sat before me again.

He leaned forward and asked, "OK, if you feel up to it, please, what did he say to you that night?"

I leaned back and thought of that cool, cloudy night. The warm crack of the fire against my cheeks and forehead.

"So," I sighed, pulling myself back from the edges of my daydream, "I was sent by the Sanhedrin to talk to your Jesus one night."

"We always thought," John said, "that you came at night so the others in the Sanhedrin wouldn't question you. That you were afraid of getting into trouble."

I laughed. My left hand dropped to press firm against my ribs.

"No, I went that night to speak for many of us at the Temple.

Was I afraid? Yes. But only of what has frightened me seemingly all my life. I did not want the Romans to see me. For if this prophet was the Messiah, we needed to prepare the people. But our preparations could not be known. Rome had eyes and ears everywhere. I had to be careful, not only for my sake but for your Jesus."

John shook his head. He leaned in toward me.

"I was in awe of you then," he said. His eyes opened suddenly wide. "I mean no offense. Even now...."

"Hush, hush," I said. "I have long been a prideful man. It has often led to my undoing and the undoing of others. I pray always that the Lord will shield me from this weakness. It seems only the weathering of old age has spared me from this fault. I no longer crave flattery, John, nor look kindly at false praise."

"I understand," he said. "What I meant is that when you arrived, I was not yet twenty years old. Here you were, coming to speak to my teacher."

"Do you remember him?" I asked.

John suddenly let out a gulp of air and stood again. He turned, and turned again, finally sitting back down before me.

"I get asked that question all the time and as the years pass it makes me more and more upset. I mean, that's what everyone wants from me, right? They want to see Jesus as he was, and I am the last of the twelve who can provide that image. And you know what?"

He fell silent. His face was a strange blend of pain and hope.

"What?" Miriam asked quietly.

"I cannot see him. Not as he was back then. I know you don't believe this....but I saw him again. Alive. Resurrected from the dead. I know I saw him on the cross, as you did. Like you, I touched his cold, bloody body. I saw where he had been buried, the stone rolled down to cover the mouth of the tomb. And then, all I can now see and hear of him is what he looked and sounded like after. I suppose it's like asking a parent of a grown child to tell you exactly how their son or daughter looked and sounded like when they were five years old."

"Well," I said, trying to calm his anguish. "That is why you are here, is it not? Maybe you can see a little of him again through my memories, what they are."

John reached out and placed a hand gently on my forearm.

I tried to remember what that night was like. What he was like. "I came to him that night with words of flattery of my own. I told him we all knew he came from the Lord, which of course most of my fellow Rabbi's did not believe. And after a while, I gathered the courage to finally ask him why he had come. Would the kingdom be reestablished through him?"

John laughed. He nodded. "We asked him the same thing many times, believe me."

"Alright," I continued, "he said to me, 'the Kingdom of God you think you seek cannot even be seen unless you are born again.'"

I paused. I looked at Miriam, and she at me. Her eyes were alight.

"No, maybe not exactly those words. But he was not interested in talking to me a moment longer about a kingdom for our people, in the here and now. He did not seem especially concerned about the Romans at all."

"I do remember you looked a bit put off by his answer," John said, raising an eyebrow toward me.

"Yes, I suppose I was not used to anyone speaking to me like that. I made what I guess was a sarcastic response to him. 'How can an old man be born again?' I asked."

"You remember what he then said? I was so impressed that he, my own rabbi, answered you like that. I repeated what he said for weeks afterward."

"Yes," I said. "He said, 'flesh gives birth to flesh, but the spirit gives birth to spirit.' And I think I was OK with that, I knew what he meant. There are plenty of Jews, flesh-from-flesh, among the descendants of Abraham who seemed to have no respect for the Lord. The Spirit of God must guide all of our faith and efforts."

"But then," I said, "he said something I could not believe. 'The wind blows wherever it pleases,' he said. 'So, it is with everyone born of the Spirit.' And then he said the one thing that kept me away from him, and you, until the week of his crucifixion. He said, 'you will not accept our testimony.' And then he said, 'the Son comes so whoever believes in him is not condemned.'"

"What was that supposed to mean, John? What? I was not only a son of Abraham, not only a leader of the Chosen People, I also followed God's every command. And yet not only was he denying the need for us to have our own kingdom again, but he seemed to claim then that this kingdom of the Spirit was to be given to whomever chooses to believe. Even more - he was saying people like me would not accept his testimony. Will not the Lord bless me for the faithful life I lived for him? Will he not lead me to truth? Was I to remain condemned while others are forgiven?"

We sat in silence then. John closed his eyes and his head tipped back. A small smile touched the edges of his mouth. Perhaps he was able to see Jesus again as I told my tale. Perhaps this was what he had sought from me in the first place.

"What did he mean?" I asked. "I have wondered about this for almost four decades. What did he mean?"

After a minute or so, John nodded to himself. Then, without opening his eyes, he said, "I will show you. You shall see. *'May the Lord give sight to the blind.'*

I gasped as he quoted the great psalm. I found myself leaning on my elbows, trying to get closer to my visitor. My arms shook under the weight of my diminished frame. Miriam rose and interlaced her fingers before her lap, noticing that I was straining myself. Perhaps. *But*, I thought, *I don't have long, so perhaps a bit of straining might be nice.*

I waited for a minute, maybe two. John seemed lost in thought. His lips moved silently as if he was reciting his Lord's words to himself.

"My friend," I said. "I don't mean to interrupt. But before the day gets too late, let me also tell you about the first time I met your teacher. It was when he was a boy, maybe around twelve years old."

John opened his left eye and looked at me, his mouth open within his beard. His hands flexed at his sides and I could see the muscles in his forearms shift under his skin.

Anna walked into the room then, glancing at Miriam in a moment of concern. I looked at her and remembered she wanted me to go to the Temple this day.

"Actually," I said, pushing myself up straight, "perhaps I can simply show you instead of telling you. Let us go to the Temple together. You must, of course, remain hidden, we'll just walk a bit in the shadows. But a walk with you and my daughter will do me good, and it may be fun to tell you something of your Jesus that happened long before you even met him."

Chapter 6
The Temple

We waited until late morning to leave for the Temple. By then the Pharisees and scribes were occupied by their chores within the inner courts. I dreaded the thought of being stopped with another set of inane challenges by those who were merely children when I was among the leaders of our people. This would not be comfortable nor safe, especially if anyone recognized my guest.

The outer court would be pleasantly busy, though nowhere near the pitch we would experience in just a couple of weeks during Passover. If we stayed in the Court of the Gentiles, John's Ephesian clothing would not look as out of place.

Anna looked at me when I pulled on my me'il. I usually wore my priestly cloak when going to the Temple, but it wouldn't help today in keeping our visitor secret. I did wear my heavy camel skin sandals, however. I rarely wore these, for they have grown heavy these past few years, but if we walked further today than I hoped, they would much softer on the soles of my old feet.

While the temperature was still relatively cool in the morning this time of year and light clouds blew through the crystal blue sky to disrupt the sun, all of us were sweaty by the time we reached the East Gate. John grew uncomfortable the closer we came to the Temple, rubbing his hands before him. I too felt the unpleasant spin of nerves. His uneasiness, however, was soon overcome by the massive walls before us. His lips parted and his eyes opened in wonder.

There was only one major gate into the Temple on this eastern side. Far off behind us rose the Mount of Olives, and behind those hills were the normally dry valleys in which we had long owned several vineyards. The land to our right rose steadily, climbing more even with the heights of the Outer Walls at the northern end. This was where a small but intimidating camp of Roman troops reappeared with the milky dawn about two months earlier. Abram and his company of guards initially built a camp between the Romans and the East Road, but later decided to pull back as close neighbors sometimes become the quickest enemies.

To our left, southward, the level of the land and the road ringing the Temple wall descended. If my legs were much younger, we would have gone that way to enter the Temple from the main Huldah Gates. However, the staircases there were not only long, but wound back and forth. Worse, the width of each stair was different to make it difficult to storm the Temple and I had in recent years been prone to stumbling upon them. I always enjoyed the decorations inside the lower-level Temple tunnels leading to those gates by which most of my countrymen normally entered and exited, but the thought of having to then walk back up the road to get to our home was too much for me.

As we approached the East Gate, several guards, dressed as Abram had been at my home the day before, carefully studied each person entering. To the right and left, shirtless men were setting up interior barricades of hay, stone and sharpened logs. These would guide the tens of thousands of pilgrims and their livestock soon arriving for the feast. Since we expelled the Roman garrison from Jerusalem several years earlier, the scope of the Passover sacrifices had grown tremendously. Though still two weeks away, already some of the tamer animals and their tenders moved into the stalls beneath the Temple. Massive loads of dry hay and grain, and thousands of gallons of water were loudly hauled into the Temple each day by young men just entering manhood.

Already, even here still outside the gate, the scent of the Temple which I had deeply embraced as a student scribe filled my mind.

The Outer Wall stood roughly forty feet above us as we passed through the gate. The sun was instantly shadowed, and my eyes fought to adjust. Anna squeezed my arm as she always did when we entered this Holy place. John kept pace, in silence, steps behind.

We entered the Court of the Gentiles. Directly ahead was the Beautiful Gate, which entered onto the Court of the Women. Anna and I agreed we would bypass this route. We turned directly to our left and walked down the long portico in the eastern wall. One set of columns, perhaps as high as three men standing upon each other, were half-embedded into the outer wall. Further into the Temple, two additional rows of free-standing columns stood, all three rows supporting a high and elegant ceiling. I eased Anna toward the outer wall and then paused. She and John came close, I suddenly realized, with a bit of alarm.

"It's OK," I said. I closed my eyes. "Just breathe."

I let the air come through my nose, slowly. There was a brief tickle as if I was about to sneeze, but I also caught the faint smell of Lebanese Cedar paneling covering the ceiling above.

"When I first worked here, the ceiling had only just been completed. That scent was everywhere. For me, this is like holding the vines from our old vineyards close to your face as the summer wears on."

"Yes," Anna said. "It is very nice. And look, John, look at all those beautiful carvings."

John stared above him. There were hundreds of carvings in the wood, and massive caps to each column in the Greek style. I smiled to myself. The last time John had been here, I was sure, was when he had been maybe twenty, or twenty-one. Just a simple fisherman from Galilee.

I paused for a few moments, still catching my breath from our walk. I then started down the eastern side of the Court toward the Royal Portico. This massive structure dominated the view to the south. After a few dozen paces, I angled to the right, gauging the easiest path through the people. The crowd was not overwhelming, but at my age....

I steadied my walking stick carefully with each step, making sure I did not hit the seams between the paving stones. John came beside me and offered his strong arm.

We passed into the bright sunlight. Every thirty feet or so stood a Jewish guard, finely dressed. The main difference from when I was an active Pharisee was that our guards were now armed, having taken the weaponry and armor left by the Romans two years earlier. To the far right were the Inner Courts and within them the Holy Place. Short poles stood every so often, holding signs written in Greek and Latin, warning the Gentiles to not enter.

"Over there," I motioned to John with a nod of my head.

We moved toward the western end of the Royal Portico. There, under the last rectangular opening a series of wide steps had been built. Over them, a short parapet hung out over the court to provide some shade or cover from the occasional rain. It was said that during the construction of the Temple, at least the early parts before I was grown, the rain held back day after day as the most critical work was finished, pouring only at night. This overhang was built then for the Chief Priest and his retinue to watch the progress. As much as I had enjoyed carpentry and even some stone carving at our vineyards, I am glad the inner courts were completed before I came of age. For only priests like myself were allowed to work in these areas.

"Under that arch, and upon those raised platforms," I said, "some of the Pharisees gathered during warm spring days to debate various questions about the Scriptures. The place has broad steps on which to sit, it was out of the way of the people and the sacrifices, and it faced north and was usually in the shade."

John moved toward the steps but stopped. He looked down. Only then did I notice the sound of trickling water. About twenty feet to our right, toward the western edge of the court, there was a small v-shaped indentation built into the paving stones to aid in drainage. Water ran through it now as the morning sacrifices had been completed. The blood and water usually went directly down into the ravines just inside the walls. But the priests were testing everything today prior to the additional requirements of the Passover.

John looked at me. His eyes glistened. He opened his mouth, then closed it.

"What is it?" I asked.

He stared at the water flowing by for several more minutes.

Then, quietly, he said, "The lamb has been slain. We don't need this any longer."

We stood in silence for a moment or two. I understood what he meant, and I found myself on the edge of argument. But I held my tongue.

Eventually, I felt as though we three were now being watched, and why not? A man my age just staring at the waters passing by? I touched John under his elbow and motioned for him to move to the shadow of the portico with Anna and me.

"We liked this spot," I said, pointing again at the steps. "Being here in the outer court, a lot of the younger boys and their mothers came and listened. We took pleasure passing along the faith of our people to them. The boys took great pleasure in learning from us. Let's face it, they then knew more about God's word than their own fathers. I often smiled to myself, thinking of these boys later telling their fathers what they had learned from us. I know how many discussions I've had with Miriam over the years concerning God and the Scriptures."

"Anyway, the first time I saw Jesus I was about thirty-years old," I said. I came close to the broad steps that served as our makeshift school. "I had been married about eight years, but my wife had not given birth to Anna yet. The rumors about us had begun, of course, but just a few months before this my wife, Sarah, had finally conceived. My business, the wineries, all was going very well. I provided many supplies to Herod, and even some to the Roman overseers, at a higher price, of course. But the wealth that often distracts older Pharisees and Sadducees, well, that level of wealth was still out of reach. I was able to spend a lot of time here in the Temple and felt a responsibility of sorts to teach the truth to the young."

"What did Jesus say to you?" John asked.

"Sorry," I said. For a moment I thought John considered there to be a division between us, but now he was only anxious to hear more about his Lord. "Old men like me seem to think we have all the time in the world to tell our stories."

I shook my head and thought back to those days. I didn't so much remember anything the boy Jesus had said directly. My memories were sharper when it came to what I and a couple of the other teachers talked about after the boy had left.

"Once," I said, "a boy came here with his father and he kept asking us about Bathsheba, and Ruth, and Delilah, and Bathsheba. And again about Bathsheba."

I laughed, stopping just short of a cough. I had walked up to the steps under the overhang, turned and slowly sat. I gently leaned my walking stick against the step next to me and reached out to pat John's leg through his robe. Anna continued to stand, looking up at the splendor of the Royal Portico.

"I don't know if I have ever seen a man as embarrassed as that boy's father."

John sighed, smiled and sat next to me.

"What about Jesus," John whispered, more urgently. He half turned toward me and leaned in close. I looked about the court for a few moments. There were a few dozen people moving about, but no one near.

"It's just," John said quickly, as if my short pause meant I wasn't going to tell him the story. "We all shared what we remembered of Jesus after he left. Then we were forced from Jerusalem and had to tell other people about him. We tried to explain him to people who had not seen and heard what we had. We'd write and share letters when we moved on to different areas. We'd try to read these letters and sometimes one of us would find an error and we'd write the author back to correct him. At times, several of us might get together to discuss what was being taught. It was easy because so many of us still lived who had actually been with the Lord."

He paused and took a deep breath. He turned his head to me and frowned.

"I'm the last one of us now and I want to hear all you know about Jesus, here in the Temple. Before your memories are also lost forever. Most of what I have heard came from his mother, Mary, and she mentioned once losing the Lord in a caravan. But this is a special memory, one I certainly did not expect to hear from your point of view. You actually met him before any of us had even heard his name. Well, in my case, before I was even born."

"Well," I said, "I have told this story once before. A long time ago a fellow Pharisee came to me, after Jesus' crucifixion. He had come to believe and follow your ways. He wanted me...."

Anna turned toward me. I didn't look at her, but I could sense her alarm. I had never told her any of this.

"Was it Paul?" John said.

I nodded.

"Paul. Saul. We both knew him, but I am afraid we knew two different men altogether. When I met your Paul, I was not in the mood to listen. But I did answer some of his questions. And I told him this story."

I leaned back and looked up at the colonnade. "So, it is not entirely a secret. I also told the story to Miriam and her friends many years ago. And after Jesus died and I returned here to my work in the Temple, quite a few of us discussed this time we saw him. Some insisted it was a different boy altogether, but I am positive it was your friend."

John peered at me, nodding. "Please. Please, tell me what you remember."

I closed my eyes and became, at least for a moment, a much younger man.

"Unlike the other boys I mentioned," I said, "this boy, this Jesus, came to us alone. He sat right over there," I pointed to my left, "like he had been here all his life. Most of our visitors cower in the corners for hours, just listening. But not Jesus. He began to ask questions."

"What questions?"

"No, that's not exactly right. Once in a while, we would have someone ask a question. Usually they were easy ones, for most of the people didn't or couldn't read the scrolls, they simply had heard something from someone in their family or a leader of their local synagogue and we would quickly answer them and move on."

"But this young boy, he didn't ask anything about the Scriptures. He seemed to know what was in the Scriptures and was only interested in how we had come to our specific beliefs. Do you understand? For example, he would not ask if God promised the Messiah to the people. He would ask why we read the words of the prophets and assume the Messiah would be this type of person, or that type of person. That the Messiah would do this or do that. We would answer, well, 'The Messiah will save us from the Romans and establish the kingdom'. Then he would ask us, 'What type of kingdom?'"

I fell silent and let my eyes open. For a minute or two, I stared at the spot the boy had once joined us. John stared at that point as well.

I turned to him and caught a tear in his eye.

"He was young, so maybe some of the others thought he was nervous. I did not. He spoke quietly and I could sense a deep calm and a deep knowledge. He was not ignorant as much as he was curious. About us. The others were annoyed at first. Some were frankly offended. 'Why do you misread that? How could you miss this?' he would ask about many different issues. Then one of us would snap back, trying to catch him in some difficult passage. But Jesus would smile a boy's smile and give an answer. But the answers, I don't know, it was like he was reminding you of something that seemed so obvious once you heard it. It was as if he had long studied the Scriptures. But who would have trained him?"

"John, I remember I was also offended for a while. But when I came back the next day and he was still there, I sat and spoke to him for over an hour, listening and answering what I could. And I could not then, nor now, tell you exactly how I felt. I did not yet have Anna in my life, and throughout my late teens and twenties I pretty much stayed away from young children. I guess suddenly I felt almost like a proud father to this strange young boy."

"Then, out of the blue he asked me, 'What do you think Isaiah meant when he wrote, 'The multitude of your sacrifices, what are they to me?' says the Lord?"

"Hmmm," John sighed.

I paused and listened to the sheep deep within the Temple, echoing up the stairwells from below. I breathed in the smell of the burnt offerings.

"This?" I asked, motioning with my hand. "All of this? Are these the sacrifices the prophet wrote about? Or does God mean my sacrifices serving this Temple? Which sacrifices mean little to the Lord?"

John stared in the direction of the Holy of Holies. He sat, lost in thought. I let him sit for a few minutes, moving to let the sun warm my legs. Anna sat now by my side, softly leaning her head against my shoulder.

"A bit later," I continued, "the boy's mother and father arrived and took him away."

John looked at me. He mouthed, 'his mother', and smiled broadly.

He leaned close and whispered in my ear.

"Mary, his mother. She lived with me for many years. I'll tell you that story later when we have a chance, but not here. She told me when she conceived Jesus, most of her and Joseph's families disowned them. In fact, many of their relations were in Bethlehem due to Rome's census when she gave birth, but they would not make room for her even in her time of need."

I shuttered deep inside. Anna pulled her head off me, looking at me with alarm.

"Yes, I know of Bethlehem."

"Well," John said, "it just makes me laugh to hear you say he was here without his parents. Mary told me she and Joseph were in a caravan heading home but most of the adults still wouldn't talk to her. Jesus was about to come of age. When he didn't join them for dinner, she asked the other adults and one of them actually lied and told them Jesus was in the caravan with some of the other children."

"Yes," I said, "When his parents arrived the second day, I realized I did not know where the boy had stayed the night before. When his mother came to him she was with her husband. I do not know how to describe it. I expected them to be frantic as I would have been, or angry. But their reactions were completely different. They hugged him, she questioned him and a couple of us commented upon the depth of his questions and answers. But I had a strange feeling that whatever fear or anger they felt was more for show, you know, more for our benefit than it had been for Jesus."

"And then," I said, "they were gone."

"I never heard about any of them again for nearly twenty years. Up to that point I never thought of this boy being the child Herod sought in Bethlehem, why would I? I was sure all the boys there had been, well, all had been killed. There was once a terrible slaughter there. Some thought a new King had been born under that star. I had no thought that this boy who questioned me on this very spot was the infant from Bethlehem. Not for another eighteen or so years, when suddenly we heard about a new prophet. A man who would have been a young boy or infant at the time of the slaughter in Bethlehem. I thought then that just perhaps this infant had survived and grown into that boy at the Temple. And now, this boy had become a prophet."

"New prophet?" John asked. "Jesus?"

"Jesus? No. But the prophet. At the Jordan, my son. At the river."

Chapter 7

Jordan

"He was certainly odd," I whispered to no one in particular.

I breathed deep the familiar smells of our home. I sank comfortably into my seat, enjoying the cool shadows.

I looked at Anna, then Miriam, and back to John. We spent much of the afternoon in the Temple discussing Jesus. John had quite a few questions concerning our Scriptures, especially concerning Isaiah. It was nice to regain the role of teacher. At least for a few moments, my body forgot its many aches. I was pleased I remembered so much. I still try to read the scrolls I kept and listen in the Temple each Sabbath. But nothing keeps the word of God deeply rooted in your mind like daily discussions and debates.

Anna set a table for the evening meal, knowing how hungry I would be after our long walk and discussion. The food was bland and simple as always. I cannot bite into anything tough or chewy. But neither John nor Miriam complained. Miriam, in fact, ate little. She hardly stopped talking to John long enough for him to eat.

Finally, I cut in and gave John a break long enough for him to take a drink. We might have sold our vineyards years earlier to help the widows of those who had fought the Romans but that didn't mean I failed to keep a selection of decent wine on hand.

"Who was odd?" Anna asked. She ate slowly, purposefully, as always. She rose several times from the table until all was adequately set and her family and guest were busy at the work of the meal. Now, she sat down to her duty over her own plate.

She lived here with me since the death of her husband. Safety, for both herself and Miriam, was ever the most critical thing to me. We lost much over the years and gave away even more in service to God. Still, my girls always had food, warm clothing and a few helpers to assist them when in need. I watched the lines slowly deepen around her eyes; she was of course old compared to the other grandmothers in our community. But she was still my little Anna.

"Father?" she said.

I smiled at her and turned then to Miriam and John.

"Who was odd? The one they called the baptizer," I said. "Earlier today John and I discussed the time I first saw Jesus. He was young then, visiting the Temple with his parents. But then he was gone, and we were left wondering who this child was, or would be. Many years passed. Suddenly, we heard of a prophet teaching not in the Temple but in the wilderness out near the Jordan."

"You saw Jesus at the Jordan?" Miriam asked. She leaned toward me, eagerly. "You heard the voice of God?"

John held a hand up toward her. His eyes were fixed on me. Miriam leaned back and crossed her hands in her lap, waiting for me to speak.

The voice of God? I wondered. At the Jordan? What was this new story, and what else had John told my granddaughter?

"No, Miriam, I never saw Jesus there. I heard nothing. But John," I looked at my guest, "not our friend here but the other one named John. Yes, I went out to see him."

I looked at the ceiling and remembered that long-ago bright, windless day.

"I marched out to the Jordan with five of my fellow leaders, led as always by Aaron. The trek took most of a day, so we left about an hour before sunrise. We reached Bethany just as dinner approached. We had six servants along with our group and they set up camp behind the crowds, maybe half a mile from the river. A few times as the sun set, we heard the echo of a deep, powerful voice. Once and again we heard the echo of a multitude of people calling out at once."

"Each of us spent the night recalling parts of the Holy

Scriptures. We knew what the people were now saying. That this strange new man was the one 'making straight the paths'."

"The Messiah?" Miriam interrupted. Anna leaned toward her daughter and placed her hand firmly on Miriam's forearm. John remained silent.

"No, Miriam," I said. "None of us even had that thought in mind. Not then. We only knew that after so many years the people were claiming a new prophet. It was our job to prove if he was true or not."

"The next morning, we woke early, took extra time to make sure our robes and head wraps were perfectly arranged. Then, in order of age, we walked single file to the rear edge of the crowd. There had to be a hundred people already there by the river. As we approached, they looked at us and parted to either side. We walked between them, vaguely aware of many whispers, and came to a stop twenty paces from the water's edge, standing maybe five feet above the level of the river."

"There we stood, and waited, and baked in the warming sun. Hours passed. I looked behind and around myself a couple of times. There were dozens more people arriving from all directions. Before us, the water flowed by smoothly. Calmly. There was plenty of relatively deep water there as a couple of side eddies created small swirling tubs of water."

"The hour was getting late and we spoke amongst ourselves about retiring to our camp to eat. Aaron stood smugly, I think believing his presence alone scared this so-called prophet away. But, suddenly, many arms rose up among the crowd, pointing to the river. No one said anything but the crowd moved at once toward the water's edge, all except the six of us. Soon, we stood rather alone."

"I looked about and there were a few sick people here and there, perhaps expecting a healing of some sort. One man laid flat on a mat. Another had a bloody wrap tied around his arm. Others were there with ailments, perhaps, that I could not see. Some stared eagerly toward the water. Many closed their eyes and tipped their heads back toward the sky in prayer. A few children were scattered about, their parents frantically cautioning them to be quiet.

"Then, he was there. I didn't even see him approach the river, maybe because of the color of his rough cloak. But suddenly a man with a long dark beard and camel hair clothing stood like a pillar of stone across the river. Everything grew silent. Then, a group of maybe eight young men came to stand beside this man. His disciples."

John smiled. "Yes, some I knew. A few became my friends. My brother James, God bless his soul, may have been there that day. I was too young."

I nodded. The pain behind John's eyes was all too apparent. I thought about the five friends I marched out to the river with that day. They too are now all gone. I am also now all alone.

"Well, the man looked at all of us, then threw his arms out to his sides and roared. I mean, it sounded like he roared at us. I have never heard a voice like his again. The river was thirty feet wide at that point, there were hundreds of us, and I am sure each heard him quite well."

"What did he say?" Miriam asked.

"Your grandpa is getting to it," Anna said. She looked at me and grinned.

"Sorry, my child," I said to Miriam. "As they say, 'an old mind has much to speak with old lips'. Anyway, this man took a deep breath and said, 'Repent, the kingdom of God has come near!'"

I heard my hands slap the table as I said this. My eyes grew wide as I looked at my family and friend, and I laughed.

"Sorry. Even now, the force of his words.... Anyway, he says this, again and again. Then he steps into the water and wades across the width of the river. The water made it up to his chest at one point and his progress was slow. But he would pause and look at different parts of the crowd and repeat, "Repent. Repent.' When he walked up on our side of the riverbank, he came right up in front of me and the others from the Temple. I could feel all of us trying to stand tall. He had come in deference to our position, that seemed clear, at least for a moment."

"'Repent of your sins and wash them away in the baptism of this water,' he bellowed at us, the water pouring off his robes. "Our gracious Lord invites you to be with him.'"

"Then he stopped. His arms slowly dropped to his sides. He

looked at the crowd to our left and right, and even behind us. I could see his followers move out of the water to form a semi-circle behind him. They were spread across the riverbank, their hands held up and open as if inviting the people to join them at the water's edge."

"But this John. He now turned back toward us. He walked forward, almost pounding the sand with his steps, and came up to our level of the bank. He came within only a foot or two and I felt myself recoil. Rabbi Aaron held his ground, crossing his arms tightly together under his cloak."

"'You brood of vipers!', John suddenly shouted. His eyes were wide and boiling, if you understand what I mean. 'Who warned you,' he said, 'to flee from the coming wrath? Produce fruit in keeping with repentance.'"

"The five of us held our breath, waiting for Aaron to respond. He and John stared at each other and then, almost as if this man was reading my leader's mind, he said, very quietly, "Do not think you can say to yourselves, 'We have Abraham as our father.' I tell you that out of these stones, God can raise up children of Abraham.'"

"With that, he kicked a small stone laying a few feet from Aaron. Aaron glared at the dripping wet prophet and swung away from us. Without a sound, our leader marched back through the crowd, with my four fellow rabbis clamoring behind. For some reason, I remained. For some reason, I was suddenly convinced that here was the child who had spoken with us at the Temple all those years before. A terrifying thought bubbled up; I don't know from where. Perhaps this was also the child who was supposed to have been murdered in Bethlehem. Perhaps this was the king raised again from the dead."

"This baptizer then turned toward me and repeated what he told Aaron, but for some reason I found concern instead of rage in his eyes."

"'You viper,' he said quietly, 'who warned you to flee the coming wrath. Repent.'"

I paused my retelling and long moments passed. Anna, Miriam and John sat silent, waiting for me.

Repent, I thought. *Only I know the depths of my sins. Did this*

John somehow know all about what I did those years before? Was he judging me with God's wrath by the river that day? As I stood and looked at him, I did believe he knew exactly what I had done. For a moment, I wanted to protest that since the night marching to Bethlehem, I had tried to produce fruit keeping with repentance. Did he not know this of me as well? Instead, I simple stood silent, staring into his dark eyes. Blinking back the sting of tears.

"Then what happened?" Miriam asked quietly.

I looked down at the table.

"Nothing," I said. "As I stood frozen, people came down to the water's edge by the dozens and John's helpers brought them into the water. John stared at me for several long moments. He then turned and raised a hand just a bit toward the river, inviting me to come in to wash with the others. Me, a leader of the Temple."

"So, I turned away instead. I turned away and followed my colleagues to the tent and then back to the Holy City before night fell. I left and didn't think about this man again until I heard he had lost his head by Herod's hand. But soon after that, well, soon after that baptizer had been executed, we suddenly had another prophet to contend with."

Chapter 8

Purpose

Our discussion continued on well after dinner. Anna smiled gently as I spoke. She was probably pleased to see me remain with her after dinner and not slink off to the cool darkness of my room. Miriam sat cross-legged on a cushion near John. After a while, I breathed deep and relaxed, hardly able to get a word or thought in around my granddaughter's bright questions.

Anna fetched me water for my cup and lit a fire, which was unusual for her now that winter turned into early spring. The warmth was pleasant. The steady crackling of the burning wood and dancing shadows on the walls grew mesmerizing. After an hour or so, I noticed Anna's eyes slowly move between John and Miriam, Miriam and John. She shook her head and rose. She brushed off the front of her dress and motioned to Miriam that it was time they retired to their room. My granddaughter stopped before me and leaned forward. Her long black hair was loose now and dropped down against my chest, reflecting the yellow flames from the hearth. I kissed her forehead, remembering the firebrand who just a few years before would have fought much harder for her place within our visitor's discussions. Perhaps age and the death of her beloved husband at the hands of the Romans gave her more insight than I had wished for her as she approached her mid-twenties.

John thanked Anna several times, then put more wood on the fire after my girls left the room. I shifted to an uncushioned chair closer to the blaze. John sat in a matching chair. He moved his sandaled feet closer to the flames. His little toe seemed to have been

57

lost to some long-ago accident and the nail on his big toe was black with bruising.

John stared into the fire and a grin spread across his face.

"Some of the best memories of my life were those long evenings," he said. "We'd sit under the stars, looking into the campfire. Sometimes, all twelve of us were with him, sometimes it would be just a few. When we were all there, especially if my brother James had a bit to drink, the discussions would end with loud laughter until one by one the others would fall asleep. Eventually, only a few of us and the Lord would remain awake, so often talking deep into the night. I was the youngest but even I rarely stayed awake longer than he did. Very often, we'd wake, and he wouldn't be sleeping at all. He would be out walking and praying."

"What kind of questions would you ask him?" I queried. "I imagine you fishermen lacked much training in the Scriptures."

John suddenly laughed. "Some of us could barely read! Which of course is perfect training for someone like me who is now being asked to write a great story! But many of us had at least parts of the Scriptures memorized."

"Anyway, what did we ask him? Usually not much about what he told us and the crowds during the day. Sometimes you'd feel like no matter what you asked it was a dumb question. That we should have paid closer attention when he told his stories, or that we were just dumb fishermen sitting with a man who knew the very secrets of God. No, we usually ended up asking strange things. What is the moon up there? Where does the wind start? Things like that."

The fire snapped several times as if laughing.

"We'd come up with some crazy questions as we walked from village to village. Just to see if we could ask him something that would make him laugh, or sigh. He would laugh. My goodness, would he laugh. Like he didn't care what anyone else thought of him. I guess the best way to describe it is that he laughed like a child. Even though he didn't answer all our crazy questions, it always seemed like he knew the answer."

I sat forward. "What was the most amazing answer he gave you?"

John looked and me and nodded vigorously, seeing his own

interest and excitement reflected off of me.

"He would usually just grin when we asked him the really strange ones. It became a game with us. I always wanted to know why the fish couldn't breathe in the air. But he always reminded us he came to lead the people to the Kingdom of God. His only purpose was to show us the Father."

I eased back in my chair. "That's all?"

"That's all? Well, if you knew the way he said that to us, well, you'd understood that was more than enough. At least it was for me."

"And the fish," I asked. "What did he say, why can't fish breathe in the air?"

John smiled.

"You know how bad fish smell sometimes? Well, Jesus said that we smell just as bad to the fish, and the fish are just trying to hold their breath."

I laughed, shook my head and stared into the fire.

"What was he really like?"

Miriam had asked that same question many times during and after dinner and John had told her many stories. But, he never really said much about what he was like. What kind of man he was.

I waited quietly. After a few minutes, I thought I saw the firelight twinkle off a tear in John's eye. His smile faded within his beard. He crossed his arms tight over his chest and hugged himself.

"I've been thinking," he said. "Rabbi Nicodemus, please help me. Please. I can only remember him as he was after. When he came back. When we get to be our age and you look back at your own thoughts, they seem to come from the same mind you have now, like nothing ever changes within you. Do you understand? I can no more remember how he was before he died as I can tell you exactly what I must have seemed like to another person thirty years ago. I can no longer truly remember what he was like before the crucifixion. I can barely recall his face or hear his voice. He somehow changed afterward. How am I ever going to write about the real him?"

I reached out a few inches in his direction but then crossed my hands in my lap.

"I have these wonderful young men working in Ephesus with me," John continued. "Ignatius. Maybe he sees how old I am now. He won't stop asking me about every detail of Jesus. Especially now that Peter and Paul are both dead. We waited these past months for word from Rome but with the chaos there, very little information trickled through. Ever since...well, ever since last fall there's been one sad report after another. The number of our people in the capital are growing. Wonderful. Praise God. But those close to me...."

John sighed and squeezed his fingers together. He stood, speaking quickly and covering his face with his hand.

"Polycarp! He's another. He is so passionate. So driven. When he heard Peter was martyred, it was all I could do to keep him from rushing to Rome himself. He was going to give the Emperor a piece of his mind. He probably thought he'd just walk right in, tell the royal court about Jesus, and the eagles would suddenly be abandoned throughout the world and replaced with our little fishes."

Slowly, I pushed myself up from the chair and let the fire warm my outstretched hand and side.

"Let's walk a bit. I always think better moving around."

I pulled two shawls over my garments and cinched a belt loosely around my waist. I led John through the front door and onto the street. It was well past dusk but what normally would have been a shuttered and silent street was still alive in places with the Passover preparations. But while this would have normally excited me, I felt only the growing trickle of fear.

We walked thirty paces, then turned south. The street here moved pleasantly downward until we came to another street going left and right.

"John," I said. "I think as with all things we should begin in prayer."

I paused and tipped my head forward. I closed my eyes and recited the psalm:

> *Teach me your ways, O LORD;*
> *make them known to me.*

> *Teach me to live according to your*
> *truth, for you are my God, who saves me.*
> *I always trust in you.*
> *Remember, O LORD, your kindness and*
> *constant love which you have shown from*
> *long ago.*

We stood in silence for a few moments. Then, John continued the prayer, reciting the next lines of the same psalm:

> *Forgive the sins and errors of my*
> *youth. In your constant love and goodness,*
> *remember me, LORD!*
> *Because the LORD is righteous and*
> *good, he teaches sinners the path they*
> *should follow.*

I suddenly couldn't breathe. *'The sins of my youth'*. How close to my thoughts my failings always remained. How close the faces of those young boys.

"John," I whispered. "You also can share your new prayers with me, can't you? I know we pray to the same God."

John sucked in a deep breath. "Yes, yes."

He reached out and grabbed my hand. His fingers were broad and warm in the cooling air. He bent his head and again closed his eyes.

"My Lord commanded me to pray this, "Our father who is in heaven....""

So many thoughts immediately crashed through my mind it was hard to keep hold of his hand. I have heard, and tried to ignore, the words and prayers of these Christians for decades now. But, 'Abba', he said! Our almighty God. A human being's 'father...'?

I forced myself to breathe softly and held my own eyes closed. I would not risk insulting my new friend.

"Forgive us our trespasses," John continued, "as we forgive those who sin against us."

Well, I thought, thinking back upon the one time I heard Jesus preach to the people. This prayer certainly sounded like him. I heard him say something about letting an enemy hit your cheek without striking back?

My mind was full of noisy thoughts and I didn't hear the end to his prayer. I waited in silence. After a moment or two, John released my hand. He backed away a bit and I opened my eyes.

I cleared my throat. "Easier said than done."

John raised his dark eyebrows.

"Forgiving others," I said.

"He told us the gate was narrow and our road was hard. And yet, I've found his commands are only hard if I try to force myself to live them out. When I let him do the work and I let him live through me, nothing seems hard."

"Well," I said. "Of course, this is where we will differ. I will ask how letting a prophet like Moses live through me makes the commands of our covenant with God any easier, and you will probably say your friend was not merely a prophet like Moses. And that is the one thing I cannot come to believe."

John patted my forearm as he led me along the street. A few doors were still open, letting in the cool evening breezes. We could smell the remains of many meals and hear the quiet talk of families within.

"I am not here to convince you of anything," John said.

"I thank you," I answered.

When he first arrived at my door, I did fear him. Mostly for Miriam. I trained her as if she were my very son, but her world is confused and scary now. Then, this man virtually out of a legend shows up at our door.

"John, others have written about your friend and recorded what he did, some of the things he said. Perhaps since you feel compelled to write, the Lord is guiding you to do something different. Maybe, tell instead what he did for you. What did your Jesus do for you and your fellow disciples? How did you experience his companionship, not as a prophet but as a friend? If you truly believe he was more than a prophet, then perhaps write about that as well. If he was more than a prophet, exactly what is he and what does he want his followers to do? What did he mean to the world? Why did God send him?"

John sank back against the wall. He passed out of the crisp white moonlight and I could only see his dark frame.

Long minutes passed.

Then, starting with a soft rush of sound, we heard the rise of many angry voices. The noise grew, echoing off the Outer Wall of the Temple. I stared northwest toward the East Gate, but it was closed against the night. Temple guards stood high above us on the top of the wall. What at first appeared to be only a dozen men soon counted fifty or more. One by one, the lamps outlining the East Gate snuffed out.

The sound reflecting off the wall grew and soon it was clearly coming from the boots of marching warriors. The clump, clump of heavy boots filled the streets. Above the rooftops of the homes to the north of us, a golden glow filled the misty night sky.

A person passed us quickly. He did not look our way, but held his cloak above his shins, walking with determined purpose. Another followed, then a pair of men ran by, looking back over their shoulders.

John and I looked at each other, then back again toward the north. The walls were a bit shorter as the ground beside the Temple rose higher than in the south. The massive stones, some weighing many, many tons and receding tens of feet into the Temple mount, stood angrily in the dark. Slowly but surely, the light from dozens of torches reflected off them like a false dawn.

"Romans," I whispered.

The marching sounds came from the direction of their new camp. Almost as if on cue, we heard rough voices cry out a cadence in Latin.

All around us came the clank and thud of closing window shutters and doors. High above, the cry of the Temple guard went out. A competing row of torchlights filled the top edge of the wall. Another group of our people ran toward the Romans and then gathered in a still group at the wall's base.

"Father!" I heard. "Father!"

"Anna," I said. My heart sank. What was she doing outside our home?

John reached for me, steadying me with his strong arm.

"She is alright," he said. "The Romans are not close yet. Let's go find her and get all of you back inside."

"Anna!" he shouted.

"Heavens!" I heard Anna shout back. She suddenly appeared at the end of our path, still in her sleeping gown and thin flat sandals. "Father, it's the Romans. Abram checked on us a few minutes ago. He's not on duty in the Temple but just run up from the Huldah Gate. The priests told him to make sure everyone remains calm; they don't want to provoke the Romans with Passover so near. Abram said more Romans arrived before dusk. They have been watching them from the road and from the top of the wall. Abram said there are thousands of them now. And it looks like the bottom parts of towers are being rolled in from the west."

"Anna," I said. "Slow down. Is Miriam safe?"

Anna nodded. She looked to her right, down the lane toward the Temple.

"Of course," she said. "She is at home, and Abram is staying with her. He brought his sword and shield. His friend, I can't remember his name, but he is with him. They said the Romans don't appear to be heading for our village."

"Where...?" I began to ask.

"There," John said. His voice was stern. He stepped in front as if to shield Anna and pointed down the lane. "They are there."

Much faster than I expected, the first rows of Roman troops came into sight. They were on the main road at the base of the Wall, the road that would eventually pass by Bethlehem far to the south. The first row carried poles with the banners of a legion I could not make out.

"Those must be the new ones," Anna growled. She moved forward but John raised his arm to stay her. "Look at those banners! Those Romans were here before. That's the garrison that killed Isah and Zacheri."

"Who?" John asked.

I moved to Anna and took her hands in my own. I looked deep into her face, noticing, as if for the first time in the dim torchlight, that my baby girl was now an old woman. Her eyes were sunken and dark, filled with fear and anger.

"Isah was Anna's husband. Zecheri was my granddaughter's spouse. They were killed during the uprising."

I walked to John's side, staring at the Romans marching by. They were already obscured by a thick cloud of dust. But the cloud did nothing to muffle the sharp clack of their weapons. To a man, they turned their heads toward the walls of the Temple, marching in precise rows toward the south. At least a hundred had already passed, four abreast, and the end of their column was nowhere in sight.

John looked at me. I motioned at the Romans with my hand, holding my walking stick aloft.

"Forgive them?" I asked our friend. "Them? How can we forgive them? They killed most of our family."

John reached out and gently pushed my hand down. He turned me back toward my home and with a soft push moved Anna and me toward our front door. As the sound and light of the passing troops dissipated and we came at last to the safety of my front door, he leaned close.

"And your people killed my Lord," he said. "My brothers. My people."

I stopped still. My mouth hung open, my teeth cooling in the night air. Anna opened the door before me and hustled into our home.

I looked up at John. He looked down at me. And gently smiled.

Chapter 9

Sermon on the Mount

The Romans who marched clear around the City the night before did not return using our side of the Temple. I tried to share in the anxious vigil my family kept upon the rooftop but often dozed off within the white swirls of my breath. I'd wake often, once with Miriam pressed close and holding me, always with a deeper and deeper covering of blankets. John stayed with us, despite the sideways looks from Abram and his comrade, Saul. John stood largely in silence and left just before dawn to make sure the other Jesus followers in the city were safe. He told me before leaving that he thought his people might have to soon leave the city for good.

Abram and Saul left our home with the sunrise, determined to go to the Temple whether their short iron swords and chipped shields were called for or not. Despite Anna's cautions, Miriam went with her betrothed. She reminded us that she worked each year helping the many pilgrims and animals coming in for the Passover and she wouldn't let a few armed Romans deny her this opportunity to serve. But, Anna and I both knew, her concern for Abram was not the youthful attraction she once had for Zacheri, but a deeper love for someone she felt she needed for the rest of her life.

Now alone in the silent morning, Anna laid out food and water for me, but she was too nervous to remain in our home. I retired to my bed but heard her step up to the roof over and again. From there she could probably see the Roman banners flying to the north. Eventually, she came down and announced through my door that she was leaving to visit friends in the lower town to make sure they were also safe.

I finally roused myself sometime after noon. I hoped my movements would wash away my thoughts of the discussion with John the night before, the looming threat from the Romans and, most of all, the thoughts that snapped to my attention when I heard John's reminder that my people had killed his Lord. But all that remained in my silent home were those memories. My thoughts turned again and again to one particular day, thirty-five years earlier, when I experienced the Galilean first-hand. I sat beside the plate Anna had left me, already exhausted. I closed my eyes and rubbed my forehead.

What had he said back then? What did his words mean to me? And, what did he do that only I witnessed?

A year or so after Herod took the head of the prophet John, I and my fellow Pharisees heard stories of someone else preaching far to the north. Had we not already heard some details about Jesus at that point, perhaps we too would have believed the wild rumors circling Jerusalem that the baptizer himself had been brought back to life. What mattered to me was only that, for the second time in a year, I had to leave the comfort of my studies to trek into the wilds far beyond Jerusalem.

The same group of six which visited the baptizer at the river now moved through the Temple gates and turned northward. Aaron still led the way, trying his best with a very ill-tempered and particularly smelly mule. We passed by the quiet little streets I now call home and eventually skirted the edge of Samaria on our way north to Galilee. As the accents of those we met became rougher and deeper, the stories we heard about this new prophet grew ever stranger.

As we moved along, I wondered. I once found a young boy in the Temple who made me think he might be the same child I thought I betrayed to his death in Bethlehem. Then, I thought the young boy had returned as the man preaching at the Jordan River. Now, we were about to face another 'prophet', this time preaching in the back lands of Galilee.

"Herod killed the man at the river," Aaron demanded one night early in our trek. "This new preacher cannot be him. Did not we also hear rumors of this Galilean before Herod killed John?"

Yes, some said. No, said others. One bold young scribe who came with us said he heard this new 'prophet' had made bread for thousands from a single crumb and had healed many of their illnesses. If he was actually John brought back to life by the power of God, I offered, would not that explain his miraculous power?

"No," Aaron growled. "This cannot be the same person. The man at the river was not a man of God, speaking to us as he did? Even if God brought a man back from the dead, where in the Scriptures do we read that this person would receive any special powers? This preacher is just as likely to be in the service of Beelzebub."

I listened and pondered. The thought that this new prophet was the one I almost betrayed to death as a newborn, a prophet who certainly would know of my sins, was terrifying. But following four hundred years of near silence, would God send us two prophets within months of each other?

There was, of course, a second possibility. All of us within the Temple silently pondered this other option and yet dared not speak it. I knew more about the scriptures than the others, and I could see better than most the intertwining of so many threads around what was now happening in our world.

Days later, we heard, now from an eyewitness to this new 'prophet', many new stories of healings. Even recoveries from leprosy. We heard of the man's teachings, once again that he could bring food down from heaven like the manna of old. Aaron marched us ever northward, walking now that his mule simply refused to move, and he had to pay a local farmer to take the beast away. Aaron prohibited anyone in our group from speaking to the local people. Still, when purchasing our essentials, we heard over and again there was a new 'kingdom of God' at hand.

Ten days into our trip, a shallow hill sloped perhaps a hundred feet above the waters of the Sea of Galilee. As we walked along the beach toward a crowd at the base of the hill, we heard the cry of a few fisherman hard at work in their boats. Most of the small vessels had been pulled in and grounded on shore, their sails and oars safely stowed within.

Just as at the river when we visited John, when the people saw us they moved to either side. In fact, because of the remoteness of this place, the awe I sensed was even greater than at the Jordan. We reached the base of the hill and looked around in glaring silence. A few people shifted away from us, backing up along the beach as we looked at them. Others walked warily up the hillside.

I looked up. Near the crest of the hill, a group of maybe twenty men and a few women sat in a small clump. A group of children played off to the right about halfway up the slope, their parents waving time and again for them to be quiet.

My eyes were drawn away from them and toward a larger group of people to my left, on the southern part of the hill. There waited dozens of people, all perfectly silent. All obviously in some sort of pain or distress.

We pulled up our blue, long sleeve robes and strode confidently up the side of the hill. We stopped just below the circle of what seemed to be the preacher's closest disciples. Perhaps young John was there among them this day. I looked down the hill, the shore was mostly empty now. The grass of the hillside was covered with sitting people. Only the six of us stood.

I heard the sea birds and the clunk of tackle in the wooden boats at the water's edge. Even the children seemed to quiet all at once. After a few minutes, a noise rose from the crowd below and behind us.

The noise grew and I sensed someone moving behind us, walking toward the top of the hill. A man walked to my left. I glanced at him and the sun, not quite at its peak but already riding high in the sky, blazed off his shoulders, leaving his face largely in shadow.

The man looked away from me as he passed, waving gently toward the people. A pair of children emerged from the crowd and ran toward him. He paused and ruffled the hair on both the children's heads. I could hear him laugh. I remember thinking there was nothing special about the laugh. Yet, there was a calmness, and perhaps a cleanness of some sort I seldom hear.

The man resumed his steady walk up the hill. I followed him with my eyes, noticing now that Aaron, slightly above me and to my right, had not even turned his head toward the man. His arms crossed before him, hidden under our long-sleeved priestly garments.

As the man walked through his seated followers, one of them reached out and touched the back of his robe as he went by. He took a few more steps, still not quite at the top of the hill, and turned to face the sea behind us.

He seemed to look directly at me and smiled. The face was young, the beard short and dark. But it was his eyes that garnered my attention. Eyes I had seen before. Perhaps, the eyes of a young boy I once met in the Temple.

I breathed out slowly. I was relieved, for this certainly was not the man from the Jordan reborn. His face looked similar, but I did not need to hear his voice to know this man was as gentle as the baptizer had been stern. This man on the hill, this Jesus, indeed might be a prophet, I thought, but he was not a man brought back to life. That shocking claim was still years away from our people.

The other option I had worried about also faded from my thoughts. This was only a man. Not a king, not a warrior to drive away Rome. This man, he certainly was not the Messiah.

He motioned to the crowd to sit. They did so, leaving us once more standing alone. He began to speak, and though he did not shout his surprisingly deep voice was certainly heard all the way to the water's edge. The huge crowd grew still. Even the noises from the fishing boats seemed to fade. A cool breeze blew over the top of the hill and gently into our faces.

At first, I did not know what he was talking about. Was he continuing something he had begun to teach the day before? He told the story about a man who had been waylaid and robbed on the deserted path. He mentioned a 'priest' and at this my attention was captured completely. Then he mentioned a Samaritan and I was even more drawn to his story. A Samaritan?

He told how a Samaritan stopped and helped a Jew who had been robbed. Then, abruptly, he stopped his story and turned his attention toward Aaron. He tilted his head and asked, "Who acted like this man's brother?"

I replayed the words of his story again through my mind. What did he say about the priest, and also about a scribe? Were there not three people in his story who passed the injured man?

Aaron, being closer and above me, had listened even more intently than I. He turned round to the rest of us, his eyes ablaze.

"He insults us," he said. "He dares insult us, comparing us with Samaritans."

With that, he pushed by me and stomped down the side of the hill. Ebener and Josiah followed him, as they always did. Oren, however, remained for a moment by my side. He also heard what my own thoughts were now just piecing together. This Jesus had indeed told the crowd neither the priest nor the scribe had helped the injured Jew. Only a despised foreigner had.

"The Samaritan," Oren answered Jesus' question aloud. Jesus looked steadily at him. The breeze flapped at the bottom of his robes. The crowd remained tense, many leaning toward Oren and this strange young rabbi to hear their discussion.

Oren bowed his head after a moment. He turned toward me and paused, but my sight was fixed on the man above. Oren shook his head with a grunt and followed Aaron down the hillside.

Jesus watched him go. His eyes were suddenly dark and sad. Then, he slowly turned his gaze to me. For a moment, it seemed as though the entire crowd had vanished but the two of us.

Slowly, perhaps to shift his eyes from me, I lowered myself down and sat on the grass. And listened.

An hour passed during which I had contemplated the rabbi's words. Now, I sat almost alone on the hillside. None of my brethren had returned. The disciples of Jesus had moved over the hilltop when their leader finished and were now out of sight. I heard a couple of people ask if Jesus was coming back to provide fish and bread for the noon meal. After a while, even these people stood and walked down toward the sea, I suppose to find lunch from another source. The smell of several fires, cooked fish and various breads, wafted up from below.

By the time the wind eased and the hot early afternoon sun beat down upon me, I sensed someone else. I turned my eyes southward and there, edging out from behind a dense thicket of bushes, was a man. At least I thought it was a man. The person wore a thick, battered cloak, with a deep hood fully covering his face even in the heat. This person moved onto the hillside cautiously. He, or she, reached down to steady themselves against a rock and slowly sat upon a flat stone on the edge of a patch of open grass.

I caught glimpse of the person's black and scabbed arms coming out of the bottom of their short-sleeved tunic.

"Leper," I whispered to myself, very quietly.

The leper pulled its knees up under its chin and looked toward the top of the hill. For the briefest moment, I saw the person's face within its hood. Torn, little more than a patchwork of folded and blackened skin. A cheek bone stood out beneath a sunken eye.

Together we sat, maybe twenty strides apart. I felt deep sorrow for this person and yet I caught myself thinking about the direction of the wind. Was it blowing across this person and toward me? My hands started to itch. I pictured myself with perfect clarity taking the long road back to Jerusalem by myself, suddenly unclean and incapable of carrying out my priestly duties. But I could not move. I sat still, as if trying to hide from a wolf that had not yet sensed me.

I peeked toward the seashore, concerned someone may come up after finishing lunch. Several families had gathered to the north. Men ate and spoke in enthusiastic debate. A few of the fishing boats had cast off, their bare-backed owners evidently willing only to lose a half-day's worth of catch. Farther off to the south, I caught the familiar blue robes of my companions. They too seemed hard at work in argument.

I thought of traipsing down the hill after the others. Instead, I turned to look at the leper again. Why was he, or she, here? Where did this person hide while Jesus spoke for over an hour to the crowd, telling us to be poor in spirit and forgiving, even to our enemies, to become peacemakers?

Behind the leper, I now saw the top of another hood, this one newer and cleaner. More of the hood rose above the roll of the hill, then the shoulders of a man walking around the hillside at the same level as the leper. I leaned forward, staring in disbelief. I brought my hand up to cup my mouth, ready to shout out a warning.

The hooded man continued toward the leper until he stood directly above him, or her. He looked down, shading the hot sun from the leper's face with his own body. The stranger then pulled back his hood. My mouth dropped open. There stood the man who had just been teaching us. There stood Jesus. All alone. Or, not all alone. The leper sat directly at his feet.

The diseased person began to shake so hard I could see the cloth of his cloak and hood move. I heard soft, painful sobs roll toward me over the grass. I quickly looked up the hillside, then down, then over my shoulder. No one was near. Not even Jesus' disciples were in sight.

I looked back just as the leper reached out with a cracked and scabbed hands to tightly grip Jesus' leg. Jesus did not pull away. Instead, he leaned forward and covered both sides of the leper's head in his hands. He smiled and then, very gently, squatted down until his face was almost directly across from the other. He said something, I could not hear what, and then his hands moved slowly back, pushing off the hood and exposing the leper's head and face to the sky above. I half turned my head and closed my eyes, expecting to see the worse.

"I believe," I heard the leper cry out in a high, shrieky voice.

Jesus said something else and lifted the man's head from under his chin. He looked the man square in the face. He smiled and my heart jumped.

Jesus looked directly at me then and motioned back toward the leper with his head. The leper turned his face and I saw it. His face was dirty, his hair matted and tangled in places down to his shoulder. But his skin was clear. His nose and ears intact. I fell back upon the grass. When the leper saw me, he shook his head in wonder. Jesus pointed at me and I suddenly knew. I was a priest and he was sending the healed man to report to me, for he was now clean. He was now clean!

The man came to me but even later that day I couldn't remember anything of our meeting but his obvious joy. I looked away from him a couple of times, but Jesus had already left. After a few minutes, I rushed down the hill as fast as I could without falling and quickly found my colleagues. I said not a word, received Aaron's scolding in silence, and insisted we return immediately to Jerusalem.

I returned to the Temple having witnessed something I could not explain. Still cannot explain. I tried to talk myself out of seeing it as a miracle but there could be no mistake. And I wondered the entire way south to the Holy City, was this man more than a mere prophet? There was one foretold in scripture who would come to heal the people. Was this he?

Chapter 10

Miracle

The next day promised to be like all those before it. Until I heard the crashing against my front door. Anna cried out from the kitchen. I rushed as quickly as I could from my bed before my swollen knees remembered themselves.

Gasping for breath, I made it to the front door just as a second heavy knock echoed within my home. I slid open the bolt and exposed the bright sunlight from the lane. John stood there, one arm hooked under the chest and arm of a second man. Large red drops of blood fell from the bottom of John's beard.

"What is it?" Anna shouted. Miriam entered the room behind her mother.

"Come in," I told John. I stepped back and the two men stumbled out of the street.

"Sorry to come here," John gasped. "Don't want to cause trouble."

Miriam rushed past me and grabbed the man next to John. I heard rough shouting in the lane as I slammed the door shut.

"It's OK," Miriam said to the stranger. She eased him onto a cushion and pulled a cloth from the table. She placed it upon the man's forehead where a dirty splotch of blood formed a deep red arc.

"I am sorry," John said again. "We were attacked by some of the younger Temple guards."

"Oh, no," Anna said.

She pushed passed me and grabbed the cloth from Miriam's

hand. She wet it with the water from the cup she laid out for my breakfast and knelt before the stranger to softly wipe his brow. She looked up to John. "They are fools! Come, Miriam, John is also cut. Bring him another wet cloth."

"It's OK," John said. He looked at his companion, worried. "They are just spooked by the Romans. They ran toward us and shouted that if they took us to them the Romans would then go away."

As I looked at Anna's crinkled brow, her lips quivered. I was sure she was suddenly thinking of her late husband, himself murdered by the soldiers of Rome. After that, she moved under my roof and I had been pleased, even in my old age, to provide her the security she required.

She tended the two men's wounds, neither of which seemed too dire. The stranger stood after a few moments, thanked us, and virtually ran out our front door, edging as far away from me as he could on his way.

To distract John from his wounds, Anna asked him about his town, Ephesus. He regained himself from whatever befell him in the alleys outside my home and now seemed entirely pleased to share some stories, many of which painted himself as a Galilean in an awkward light, trying to deal with all these foreign people, and a new culture, near the Aegean Sea. I stood slowly, grimacing in anticipation against pain that thankfully would not return at all that day. I eased open the window shutter by our front door to make sure no one waited for my guest.

"Don't tell my father," Anna laughed behind me, "but I had to deal with a lot of Gentiles when we sold our wines. I'm just teasing, obviously he knows. He also had to handle this trade himself, and deal with the Romans too, if you can believe it. My father was a great man, a great and holy man years ago."

I squeezed my lips together over a smile. The edges of my eyes stung with the start of a tear.

"I know a lot of his colleagues in the Temple did not like him," she said, "or at least did not like our wealth. But I will tell you, I never met anyone who gave away so much to those in need as my father."

"Yes," John said. "There was a man who met me in Ephesus once. Joseph. He told us your father actually helped him bury my Lord and spent quite the fortune doing so."

"Yes, yes," Anna said quickly. "He told me parts of the story once. That was a difficult time in Jerusalem. My father lost a lot when your Lord died."

"Well, at least he has you," John said.

"Yes," Anna said. "I wanted to go back to our vineyard then, and again after Iseh was killed. He was my husband. I wanted to get away just to clear my head. Wanted to leave behind all my memories. But my mother died of the fever not long before, so my father needed me. He was not young when I was born, and I was not young when I gave birth to Miriam. So, we all need to stick together."

I pressed my hand against the inside of my front door and closed my eyes. Anna and John fell silent. I hadn't thought of Anna at the winery for some time. We had just sold it two years earlier for funds to help supply the Temple after the Romans were forced out. Anna never complained about it. Never told me she thought of going back.

"Father?" she called.

I closed the shutter tight, sure now that the lane was clear. I turned to John, checking his bruised face.

Anna stood and went into the kitchen. John stood politely until I sat. He turned to me and waited as I took a moment to position all my aching limbs on my cushions.

He asked me then to go with him to Bethany. He said he wanted to walk first to the Mount of Olives but did not want to go alone so as to rouse suspicion.

Anna rushed back into the room and would have none of it. While the Mount was on the eastern side of the City, Bethany sat some way further away from the sea. Not too great a distance from our humble home, except that the Roman outpost was growing. While there had been no further probe as there had been two nights earlier, the City was on edge, nonetheless.

Also, she reminded us, the roads and hillsides in that area were already filling with those arriving for Passover with their sacrifices.

John looked at Anna, then at me. He had come to our home days before like a young child hoping against hope for some sweet treat from his mother. As we discussed the words of his Lord these past days and the grind of leading his people in Ephesus receded for a moment, I could sense the years of concern falling from his shoulders. In the end, I think he now knew I had sincerely considered Jesus and in the years since his burial tried to live by much of what he taught.

I had given when asked, I always asked others how I might help. Each time I helped, I would feel, at least for a while, as if I had pleased God. I thought once, when I sold my home in the upper city to pay for engravings in the Temple, perhaps God would someday truly forgive my sins. Then, as the long years ate away at me, I gave up and simply waited for death, hoping God might simply look upon me with final compassion.

John didn't want to simply walk the hills he probably had walked decades before with his friends. There was no mistaking that, in John's mind at least, time was growing short for him to accomplish his task here. Since the Roman incursion, the thoughts of those lost to the Empire were never far away. But, with Passover almost upon us, what could the Legion possibly do?

John thought perhaps he had something more important to show me in the fields. Or, perhaps he thought he might gain the knowledge that he sought from me under the sun of the day. At first, it seemed, my Anna would not let that happen. *Probably*, I thought, *for the best.*

"No matter, Anna," John finally said. "How about just a short walk in the garden. Come with us, please."

"That's still in the direction of Bethany," Anna said.

He looked at Anna and held his open hand out to her. "I promise. We won't go far."

Anna looked down at the table. I knew she was considering both my safety and the chores beckoning her to finished. She leaned on her fists, pressed firmly against the tabletop, raised her eyes to our guest and nodded.

"OK," John said quietly. "I will not go far with your father. We will be back before noon."

I followed John through the door and into the street beyond. I enjoy blue sky, but I also now fear the heat of the sun more and more as the years pass. Fortunately, there was a cool breeze puffing from the north. John pointed to the reeds growing tall right and left of our path.

"Do you remember?" he asked. "About a week before the crucifixion. Do you remember?"

"Of course," I said. "The week of Passover was upon us then as it is now."

John nodded. He turned toward me and looked over my shoulder.

"I wanted to go to Bethany," he said. "For that is where we all saw it. There is where we watched as Jesus raised a man, a man named Lazarus, from the tomb."

I nodded. I had heard the story, we all had, so many years ago now.

"Some say your friend did many miracles. I think I actually watched him heal a leper, though my memories have grown dim. But the miracle you speak of? Raising a man from the dead? If true, it was his greatest miracle of all, I am sure. But it was also the moment so many other plans set into motion. I am sorry, I don't think I have the energy to tell you that story right now."

John chuckled. He gently patted my shoulder.

"That's more than fine. Oh, Rabbi Nicodemus," he said lightly. "Lazarus. We had been with him just a few months before. When he stumbled out from that cave! I remember his little steps, like a child, the wrap was so tight around his body. Walking toward us on legs once cold and dead. His poor sisters, they were beside themselves. One of us, I'd say it was Judas, of course, but I don't remember for sure, went to Martha and demanded to know if her brother had even been dead. Can you imagine? But there could be no doubt. He had been in that tomb for days."

I looked at John, gripping the top of my walking stick hard. I heard the stories just days later as this event spread throughout Judea. It was something you couldn't deny, and yet couldn't really allow yourself to believe either. I mean, if you believed this, what else would you have to believe?

So many people who saw this supposed miracle with their own

eyes came to Jerusalem for that year's Passover, no one could avoid the story. You could walk the streets and be practically knocked over by a storm of excitement. The entire city was in chaos. I watched from the Temple wall as a mass of people, shouting and waving and tossing palms into the air, squeezed out of the gates to meet Jesus when he entered Jerusalem. Riding a donkey, no less!

"Yes," I whispered. "His greatest miracle."

John blinked, seeming to come back from the world of his memories. He looked deep into my eyes.

"Oh, no. No, that was not his greatest miracle. Not at all."

John pointed to the ground a few dozen yards from us, a small patch of garden called Gethsemane.

"His greatest miracle was not raising Lazarus, good teacher. It was just over there, in that garden. There is where his greatest miracle began."

I shook my head. For just a moment I felt somehow threatened, almost as if my lack of faith was placing me in danger next to my larger friend. I knew full well what John believed, but I wasn't going to put it in words. Words that might lead us into an argument.

John looked high to the top of the Temple Wall and pointed as if to the far side. Toward the hill. "And it ended way over there. On that cross."

"His death on a cross was a miracle?" I asked.

"Yes," John said. "Of course. The agony that began here ended on a tree on the other side of the Temple. He died there as a sacrifice for our sins. The sins of the whole world. The lamb of God. He sacrificed himself, so we may be with the father."

My back stiffened.

"And yet, the real miracle happened the morning of the third day. He rose from the dead. No, father Nicodemus, his greatest miracle, the only one that ever made any real difference, was that he brought himself back from the dead."

I shook my head and looked away from the garden.

John looked at me, calm and gentle as ever.

"It wasn't the father working through him," John said. "Don't you understand? He told us. We didn't understand his words, but he told all of us very clearly the last night we ate together. He told us he was laying down his life for us. He told us he would take his life up again. He told us he sacrificed himself, willingly, as our friend. And that he had the power to bring himself to life again. That, my good rabbi, was the true miracle. On the third day this man, dead, raised himself back to life again."

We stood and looked at each other for several long moments.

"And then," John said, "he walked among us, all of us who had failed him and abandoned him and cowered away in fear. And he, our Lord who had power enough to raise himself from the dead, he who had the power to give life, even to himself.'

John raised his eyes to the sky.

"He who showed us he possessed the very power of God, came among those of us who should have been willing to die for him. And he forgave us all our sins."

Chapter 11

Meeting

Later that night, John and I sat in the small courtyard behind my home, warming ourselves by a fire. Anna buried me under a half-dozen blankets. Despite the covers and the fire, I was still chilled when the breezes grew from the north to push the smoke away from me.

"I was thinking last night," I said.

"What were you thinking about?"

I laughed. "Many things, my young friend. You've made me think of many things these past weeks. Things most men my age should be able to just lock away in the dark of their minds so we can die a simple death surrounded by simple and pleasant thoughts."

John pushed against one of the fire logs with the long stick he twisted before him. Dozens of flaming sparks danced into the black sky.

"The night you visited Jesus," he said, "I don't remember you being a rabbi who was troubled by difficult thoughts. I suppose that's why I sought you out. I have so much heaped upon me, and now this constant call to write about Jesus. I hoped you could steady me, help me with this task."

I moved my arm to reach out for him, but found the blankets laying upon me too heavy.

"I know what you mean," I said. "I only met your friend a few times and yet over the decades I occasionally tried to decipher his words to me. I've tried to figure out what I saw when I was with him. I've largely ignored your people, but I know Miriam listens from

85

time to time. She even has brought her Abram with her to a gathering, at least once that I know of. That's why I know he loves her, for I can tell how uncomfortable he was. A temple guard, going to see the followers of the Nazarene. I have to admit, I am far less than comfortable with the thought myself."

We sat in silence for a while. I can't remember what I expected John to say then. I certainly did not want to make him feel uneasy. I could see the bruising in his lower lip, though most of the swelling hid beneath his beard. He played with the logs in the fire, exposing them to the air until new flames warmed my face.

"I didn't want to bring it up earlier," I said, "you have enough trouble. But I did read some of what Saul wrote about Jesus. We all knew Saul had a brilliant mind, even if we were a bit afraid of his passion. We tried to stop him from attacking your people. I hope you know that."

John nodded. His mouth pressed tight behind his beard. "I know. He told us himself."

Good, I thought. Another dark memory I had not looked at for many years. Perhaps it was one effort I had made which was actually successful.

"After he came to share your beliefs, I asked him to come here. Well, not exactly here. We met out in my vineyards, far from prying eyes. He was anxious to explain the wisdom of his choices. Maybe at first I was hoping to turn him back to our ways. It certainly would have helped put my own mind at ease. Instead, the best we could do was reach the point where we both respected each other. I remembered he looked at my land and suddenly smiled. 'Jesus is the vine', he said. I teased him that I didn't know he was such a poet. But his mind kept spinning around that thought."

"Do you know what his main concern was?" I asked. "He visited me, I think, to make sure I agreed with how he saw Jesus in terms of what the prophets had written. I was not such a doddering fool back then, believe it or not. I was still known as something of an expert."

"I am sure of that," John said. "Everyone knew of Nicodemus."

I sat for a long moment in silence, stunned and warmed by John's unexpected compliment. After Jesus had been crucified, I was asked to teach and debate less and less often. I suppose I didn't mind. I was both angry and deeply disillusioned by what had been done. I filled my life instead with other things that brought me some satisfaction.

"Well," I coughed, "I don't know if I was of much help to Saul. If anything, I think maybe I just calmed his fears."

"Fears? Paul? He was never afraid of anything."

"Oh, yes," I turned to face my friend. "He wasn't afraid of us in the Temple. He wasn't afraid of the Romans. But he was afraid of you."

"Me? Us, you mean? He was afraid of all of us? Why?"

We sat quietly for a moment. John then hummed to himself and nodded.

"Yes. You know what he was afraid of," I said. "It's obvious. He wasn't one of you. He had never walked with Jesus. And there were twelve of you who not only lived with Jesus but walked with him after you say he rose from the dead! Even I had met your Lord in person and spoke to him. But not Paul. He had not been one of you."

"I see that, but I still don't understand why he would be afraid of us. We were the ones at first afraid of him."

I pulled my hand from under my coverings and held a finger toward John.

"He was afraid you would not accept what he claimed, or what he wrote. He believed your Jesus spoke to him as well, but he didn't know if you and the others would just laugh at him and send him on his way."

"I never....," John sighed. "I mean, it was startling when Paul first showed up, especially since we all knew what he had done in Jerusalem. And his story was certainly unnerving at first."

"More unnerving than your story of a crucified man coming back from the dead?"

"No," John chuckled. "No, and that's the point. Nothing could be more unnerving than that. But as we listened to Paul, and we discussed his message, all of us sensed he was speaking the truth. Where that led us in terms of how to deal with the Gentiles and many other issues, well, that took a lot of prayer and debate. But I don't think any of us doubted Paul for long."

"Well," I said, "Saul brought one of his letters the day we met in the vineyards and what I read unnerved me. Not as much as what I heard Jesus taught, perhaps. I was not alone in being unnerved by his words, if I remember correctly. In fact, there was a time when the Sanhedrin heard most of Jesus' followers had left him. The hope passing around the Temple at that point was that you all had left him."

"Yes," John said. "Well, not all of us left. If you were confused at times by your one meeting with him, we were all confused many times during our travels. I am sure the event you are referring to was when a number of your fellow Pharisees came to challenge him. He spoke then about things that made all of us wonder."

I turned my shoulders toward John as far as I could.

"What did he say?"

John raised his eyebrows and stared into the fire.

"You might not understand. We didn't fully understand until the Spirit later came to us, so how could you possibly understand now?"

"You mean I don't have the Spirit of the Lord with me?" I asked.

John shook his head. "Sorry, I don't mean to insult you. The thing is, Jesus told the Pharisees that day that he was the new manna, that he was new bread come down from heaven."

"Bold words," I said. "But I had heard rumors of that exact thing when we once went north to see him."

I looked back into the fire, the leaping flames were dazzling in the night. I suddenly understood I had not really asked John much about his faith since he arrived. Why was that? And he didn't seem ready to offer much. I know his people took many of my fellow Jews with them these past several decades. But John said little to me, and almost nothing unless I asked. Why?

John let the stick drop to the ground next to him. The tip, still in the fire, tossed glowing embers into the air.

"By the end of that discussion," he said, "almost everyone who had been with us left Jesus. He earlier sent out some of these same men to the towns to announce his coming, but now even they walked away. I remember glaring at the scribes and Pharisees who were there, really angry with them. I blamed them for causing Jesus to say these strange things. For their parts, your colleagues were angry with him for what he said. I even heard them call out 'blasphemer'. Others, when they saw the other disciples leave, just smiled. But there were still the twelve of us. Peter, my brother, Andrew. The others."

"Jesus turned to us and looked exhausted. He looked at each of us, one by one. 'Are you leaving as well?' he asked. I didn't know what to say. Then Peter, as always, answered. In the blink of an eye, Jesus seemed energized again."

"Why?"

"Well, you have to remember....," John started, then paused. "Look, I'm not trying to convince you of anything, but after we saw him raised to life again, he sent the Spirit to us. Everything that once seemed so strange became clear. We couldn't understand how anyone could doubt what we had seen. But I realize now that, during that day when all the others left, things were different. Jesus had not yet been resurrected. The Spirit had not yet come as he did later. So, for the twelve of us to remain, for us to follow him even when we didn't understand what he was teaching...."

John pushed himself up from his seat and grabbed another log for the fire. He turned to me, using the end of the log as a pointer to stress his words.

"God gave each of us a special gift that day. A special insight, maybe, a unique moment of faith. After the Spirit came, we understood. But at that moment, facing off against the Pharisees, the father drew us to Jesus in a special way.

"Later, when we were left to ourselves, I trembled at the thought. Out of all the people from all the ages of the world, only the twelve of us had been chosen. That day when the others left, I saw Jesus' expression change when Peter confirmed we would stay. I knew he was now confident he would go through the rest of his trials with us twelve, well eleven. His brothers, solidly by his side. I've been asked over and over how I escaped the Romans that terrible day on Golgotha when I stood in broad daylight beneath a condemned blasphemer. All I can answer is that the father protected me that day as well."

My chest ached as I eased in a shuddering breath.

I hadn't been there when Jesus' followers left him, but I had heard about the encounter from my fellow Pharisees. The thought that plagued me all those years before came back full force. How could men like this John, not the strong fully-formed man standing before me now, but the young, unworldly and uneducated John and his friends of thirty years earlier, do and teach all they have, even before the leaders of our faith and beneath the threats of the Romans? How could this Jesus, dead and buried, change so much so quickly?

I cleared my throat and struggled to pull my arms fully out from under the blankets. I saw my breath now in the night air, but I suddenly felt hot and trapped.

"In the end," I said, "it wasn't the things he said the night we met which shook me the most. Not even the time I saw him cure a leper. It was the miracle you told me about earlier. Raising his friend from the dead. Then he came to the Temple for Passover. And people were shouting that a new king was among us. I had heard that claim once before, decades earlier."

"Up to that point," I told John, "we had the authority of the scriptures, and while your Jesus may have expanded upon them, he also followed and respected them. We could hear about the miracles and healings and still be content because, certainly, attributing miracles to the power of God was fine. We were still the only ones who spoke for him on earth."

"But to raise someone from the dead," John said. He stood, head down, gazing steadily into the fire.

"Exactly. To have the power to raise someone from the dead, John, well that was a power which indicated God's power. His authority. Authority that threatened us. Power that would also threaten the Romans."

"What did you do?" John whispered.

"I once betrayed your Lord, John. Another story for another time, perhaps. But during Passover week, at the meeting of the Sanhedrin, I did not repeat my mistake. I, and a few others, we each tried to save Jesus. We truly did. In the end, we failed."

"How?"

"Because our high priest stood before us all and said, 'You know nothing. You do not realize it is better that one man die for the people than the whole nation perishes.'"

John brought his hand to his forehead and shielded his eyes.

"Rabbi?" he said.

"Yes?"

"I know Anna might not like it, but would you come with me tomorrow? My thoughts are overwhelmed by this place, by what you are saying. Everything. I want to visit the garden once more. My heart needs to walk under those trees again. It was the last time I walked with him before his death."

"Of course, John. Of course."

Chapter 12

Garden

The next morning, John led us into the garden early, before the heat of even this spring day grew oppressive. His leisurely walk gained urgency as we continued our trek. I was about to ask him to slow when, suddenly, he pulled up, standing still as a statue in the streaks of sunlight carving through the morning fog from the east.

"We came here that night," "Four of us. We sat right there, under that tree."

He pointed to a small gnarled tree a few feet away. The outline of what looked like a fish had been carved into its tough hide. At the base, the bark and roots receded, forming a perfect seat. He stepped toward the tree and reached out to steady himself, leaning against the tree's bark, looking up into the budding branches. He squatted and stared at the curve near the base of the tree.

I scanned the low olive trees and the early spring flowers around us. I faced downhill, toward the south. The Temple loomed to my right. Behind us lay the many quiet lanes surrounding our home. Beyond that, the Roman encampment.

The garden was almost empty, and there was an eerie quiet. Eerie because large groups of pilgrims should have been coming for Passover this day, moving along the East Road. The following evening would bring the silence of the Sabbath and then the Holy City would truly be overrun during Passover week.

But there was hardly a sound from the north. We could just make out the East Gate and a band of Temple guards at the base of the wall. Other than that, very few people or animals moved toward

93

the gate.

"I wonder what's going on?" I said.

I noticed Anna and John look at each other with concern for a moment.

"Anna?" I asked, suddenly thinking of Miriam.

"Before you woke," John said, "we heard more Romans are joining the camp. That man, the guy with the cedar walking stick at the end of your lane, he said a barricade had been laid across the East Road. Some of the Romans seemed to be stopping the pilgrims and taking their animals for themselves. Miriam went to find Abram, she thought he was called again to the Temple."

John pushed himself off the tree and wandered slowly around its base.

The early spring breeze was cool and pleasant, but my thoughts were dark.

"They wouldn't dare," I whispered. "Not during Passover."

Anna and I walked to John, careful not to trip on the interlocking roots within the garden just barely covered by rough grass.

"Why were there only four of you?" Anna asked.

"Oh," John sighed. He reached up for a low hanging branch and caressed the limb like the cheek of a young child. He looked through the branches, then leaned back to look further into the sky. The veins of his neck stood out below the edge of his beard.

"Jesus often took three of us aside. Not entirely sure why," he sighed heavily. "Sometimes I suppose it bothered the others, but when Jesus did something you tended not to get too upset. Peter was one of us, of course."

He paused and repeated, "Peter". His head tipped forward and he closed his eyes.

"I heard of his death just last year. Have you ever met someone who just seemed to be so there, so solid, so alive, that you can almost believe they will never die?"

I nodded. Even though most men in my world had grown slow and 'proper' with age, I knew a few who seemed virtually immortal. Fires that never seemed to be quenched.

"Jesus also included me and my brother, James. Peter was

actually Simon, I'm sure you've heard that. Jesus renamed him Peter. By the time of the crucifixion we all called him that. As for James and I....well, I guess we were both head-strong and a bit obnoxious. He told us once he should change our names to 'thunder'."

Anna chuckled softly, "I think I would have liked to have met him."

A cold finger traced up my spine and I shook. I had never heard Anna say anything of a religious nature that did not adhere strictly to our faith. Miriam would question and question and question as I taught her, and often she would ask me questions that made me go back to the scrolls. But never Anna. For all I had ever heard, she held the Nazarene in utter contempt.

"That night," John said, snapping my thoughts away from my daughter, "Jesus walked over there."

He pointed toward a small rise. A pair of old bushes seemed to make an arch of sorts, though the bushes looked to be dead. Even as the rest of the Garden began to flower, only a few dark brown leaves clung onto their branches.

"He went there, off by himself. I can barely look at it still. I haven't been here since that night. Quite frankly, I almost feel as if I should remove my sandals, like Moses. We are truly on holy ground."

It felt as if the air had fallen still and I found it hard to breathe. My body felt heavy, as though I was pressed against the earth.

"There was no one here that night," John said. "All were celebrating Passover. There were some torches passing back and forth by the Temple, and a few above on the wall. But here it was only the moonlight lighting the hill."

John stopped and brought a hand to his beard. He shook his head slowly, his eyes tearing just a bit. He looked at me and held my gaze. A smile fought for space upon his face.

"I can see him," he said. "I can see him! Rabbi, here in this place, I can see him. Not like after he came back, but just as he was that night. I can see his face!"

"He told us to pray for him, to wait by this tree. He walked off toward those bushes. He came back a while later, but we were dozing. It had been a very heavy meal," John smiled. "Then, he moved away from us again. This time, Peter and James slept. "

"And you stayed awake?" Anna asked.

"Well," John said. "Perhaps not for the entire time, but Jesus had commanded us to pray, to provide him support. How could I not try? And I was young."

"But the others?" I asked.

"My big brother never shied away from a cup of good wine, and there was plenty during our Passover supper. He was 'calm', as they say, and content and full and the tree we sat under was far too comfortable. And Peter, I always teased him he was an old man. Ha! Old man? He was then younger than I am now. But, he seemed fatherly to me. Especially when he was around Jesus. Try as he might that night, he could not stay awake. He tried everything. I heard him sing to himself. He prayed out loud and even knocked his head back against the trunk. But that cool night air was too much for him. I tried to rouse him, but it was no good, and I didn't want to interrupt what Jesus was going through."

"What was he going through?" Anna asked. I glanced at my daughter. Her eyes, the moment before alight, turned dim when I looked at her and she lowered her head and backed away. I wanted to move toward her, to tell her, what? But I could not.

"He was in such pain," John said. "It was as if he was being ripped away from his own children. But, this was more. Deeper. Desire and despair and hope and sadness, more than I have ever seen. Like someone who knows they can have their deepest desires and yet they are called to give them up."

"I heard," I said quietly, asking the question I had heard Anna and Miriam discuss once after they thought I had gone to bed, "that he sweated blood."

John nodded.

"It was dark. I can't tell you for sure, it's not like we came back to check the ground when it was light. Perhaps it was just sweat mixed with dirt. But it certainly appeared to be blood. He was drenched with it, his hair matted to the sides of his face. His hand trembled when he came back to us the third time, I remember that. It was then, for me at least, when my embarrassment was complete.

When I roused myself, it was as if the world had stopped. I could hear nothing. I could see nothing in the dark but the silver light of the moon reflected in my Lord's eyes, and glistening off his sweat. It was then that he sighed, like a grunt, and looked to the ground. He closed his eyes and slowly nodded. He whispered, 'Your will be done."

"That's when we saw the torches of the Temple guards approach."

Chapter 13

Siege

John fell silent. It was now moving toward dinner, and the spring sun dipped behind the Temple, casting shadow upon us.

In my thoughts, I could almost hear the marching boots of the Temple guard that night long ago. The guards would have come for Jesus, leaving by way of the southern gate, most likely, but instead of retracing my path toward Bethlehem and slaughter, they would have marched back up the hill toward this grove.

I then realized the sound of marching was not only in my mind. Behind us, echoing off the walls of the city came the call of Temple guardsmen standing high upon the ramparts. Before I could focus upon what was happening, Anna gripped my hand.

"Look," she whispered. She pointed toward our home.

Above the rooftops, we could see the points of several poles, topped with eagles and the banners of the Roman troop. There seemed to be no motion from their camp, except for an occasional rider moving about, sometimes heading toward the Temple, sometimes out farther to the east.

Within minutes, however, a pair of horsemen passed the southmost homes. They skirted along the cobbled road hugging the Temple Wall. The echo of their horse's foot-strikes was almost deafening. Moments later, another pair of helmeted heads came over the rise, then several more. Within moments, dozens of heavily armed men road by, scarlet robes snapping in the wind. Dust swirled about their steeds' legs.

Anna moved close behind me, her breath heavy on my neck. She turned me toward her. Her eyes danced away toward the walls, then came back to hold my gaze.

I nodded toward the East Gate of the Temple.

"Miriam is safe. She's probably with her friends. Or with Abram."

Anna shoulders sank forward. "That's the problem. Miriam always thinks she'll be alright. Abram as well. He's a wonderful man, I know you think so, but he just adds to her belief in her safety."

"Anna, if you need to go find her, go. Please, don't worry about me. I will be fine."

"And I will go with you," John said. He stepped quickly over the broken ground and came to my daughter's side.

Anna stopped and held her palm out to him.

"No, she said. "You stay and take care of my father."

"Anna!" I cried. Even after the death of my son-in-law, Anna also held an unreasonable belief in her own safety.

"Father," she said. "I can't wait for you; you can't walk fast enough. I can't leave you here alone. Besides, I will be safer by myself. The Romans will have no interest bothering an old Jewish woman like me."

Anna walked off, ending any debate. Her dress caught once or twice on the brambles at the edge of the garden. Within minutes, she blended in with a caravan of a few dozen priests coming to the Temple from the villages off to the east. John stood beside me, his hand resting lightly on my shoulder.

"She is correct. She'll will attract less attention alone, and she knows where Miriam would most likely spend the day."

"I know," I said. I looked at him. "Could we wait here a few more minutes? We've seemed to have lost the quiet of this garden, but I do not think I could just wait alone in my home at this point."

John looked over my shoulder. Beyond our homes, the East Road stretched left and right. Behind that, upon the edge of the horizon, smoke rose from the Roman camp.

"We should at least start walking toward the road. Just in case we need to move quickly."

John carried my walking staff in one hand, since the ground was too rough for it to be of much help. I used his other strong arm for support. I don't know how much time passed, but we had made barely a hundred steps toward the wall. Suddenly, there was a loud boom from the right. We stopped and looked north. Even with my poor eyesight, I knew the East Gate of the Temple had been forced shut from the inside.

Outside the gate, a large crowd moved toward the Temple along the East Road and spilled north and south at the foot of the wall. A few screams echoed over us as hundreds suddenly had nowhere to go. A few among the guard had also been caught outside the Temple. I watched them, one-by-one, light fresh torches by the cauldrons burning on both sides of the gate. The torches waved back and forth; white smoke swirled into the air. Rough commands told the people pushing toward the gate to move toward the southern gates instead. More guards leaned over the ramparts above, pointing and shouting.

Suddenly, we heard the roar of drums. As they faded away, all turned deathly still.

"More Romans," John said. He squeezed my arm tighter and led me south toward a smoother area in the tall grass. Then he turned us back toward the Temple wall. I stumbled along for a few steps, then pulled John to a stop.

"Look!"

Far to the north, a large group of Romans rode down from their camp. I had not seen such a large group of mounted horsemen for years. They galloped three abreast. The middle lead horse snorted angrily and pushed the horse next to it into the wall, pressing its rider into the massive blocks for a long moment.

They came on, approaching the gate. Screams rose from the now stranded mob. Dozens of people, carts and livestock rushed after a young Temple guardsman, torch flaming high above his head, as he led them southward upon the road. Fleeing toward the Huldah gate. I pulled on John to turn around and hurry back toward the north, to our home. Toward Anna. John stood still, watching. He grimaced and nodded toward our village.

A pair of horses galloped out from the near end of one of the lanes. Then another pair from the lane to the right. Over and again, single horses, or pairs, crashed through my village. The Romans did not have their weapons drawn, but they were quite terrifying, nonetheless.

John stepped upon a large knotted root. He towered over me and I felt all of my eighty-seven years at that moment.

"Anna," I said. "Miriam! What are we to do?"

"Come," John said. "We can't go back to your home, not with Romans in the lanes. The East Gate is closed. See, all the others move south, we must follow them to the other gates. We can find Anna and Miriam within the Temple."

He scanned the road before us and pointed toward the growing shadows of the Wall. The leading edge of the crowds who had been forced south circled the Temple to find refuge through one of the other gates. John motioned toward a small cart pulled by an elderly man. The man, and his cart, were about to be overrun by those behind him who were younger and stronger. He was still perhaps a full quarter mile away from us.

John stopped and turned to me. He took a deep breath and held out his arms.

He wanted to carry me! I had not been carried by anyone since childhood, except when I snapped my lower leg nearly twenty years earlier. I opened my mouth to protest but saw immediately that I had no choice. John was right. With the East Gate closed, we would never make it to the other entrances if I walked.

I can't begin to tell how it felt to be carried like a fool across that field. John put me down twice to rest and shake out his arms, giving me back a nugget of pride. Within fifteen minutes, we crossed from the garden to the old man pulling the cart. As we approached, the man was bumped hard enough by the panicked crowd to drop the handles of his wagon.

John grunted with each step as he lifted me up to the level of the road. He gently put me down and stood for a moment, breathing deep. He waited for the man with the cart to come close. The old man had slowed considerably from the time we first saw him across the field. He looked to be in his upper sixties, dressed as one coming down from the Galilean uplands. He limped badly on his right leg and seemed close to the point of tears.

John motioned to me to walk as quickly as I could behind him, which was not very fast at all. I was almost twenty steps behind John when he stopped beside the wheel of the man's cart. He spoke a few words, motioned to me again, and turned his attention to a group of pilgrims fleeing the Romans. John held up his hand to ward off these others, placing his body between them and back end of the cart. He called for me to join him.

I rushed toward the cart as quickly as I could. By the time I came close, the cart's owner was already sitting upon the open bed in the back, facing north. John lifted me into position, sitting me next to the other man on a bale of loosely tied hay.

"This is Mathias," John said to me breathlessly. He gave one more look of warning at those coming up behind and stumbled to the front of the cart. I turned to the owner of the cart.

"I am Nicodemus," I said.

"Well met," my seat mate said. We hung on for dear life as John lifted the handles and bounced us roughly within the grooves of the paving stones.

The sun sank low by the time we fully rounded the south eastern end of the Temple. Before us raged a mass of humanity, climbing the steps toward the two Huldah gates. The smaller gate was open, but there were far too many people crammed together onto the upper porch to let anyone pass. The stairs leading to the triple gate, the one most of us normally used to enter the Temple, was an even more troubling scene. One group of four men had lifted their full cart up the stairs. The stairs tops were of different depths and this caused them to trip. Their cart seemed ready to plunge upon the people below. More than once, someone upon the stairwell was squeezed over short walls and forced to jump from ten or even fifteen feet above. A double ring of armed Temple guards created a buffer at the top of the stairwell, letting only a few through to the gate behind.

John assessed the impossibility of making it into the Temple from this direction. He dragged the cart forward, passing Potters Field to our left. Sweat stained dark the back of his shirt. As we rounded the tip of the Temple and the road rose again, John bent forward and yanked us along with a mighty grunt. The top of the wall, here looming maybe fifty feet above us, was a darkening orange in the fading afternoon light.

Before us was the Coponius Gate, perhaps a third of a mile away. Despite John's weariness, his steps quickened. There were two long lines of stalls and shops, lining both the outer edge of the road and set back against the Temple wall. The shop owners scurried about, tying down what they could and generally getting in John's way.

As we came within a few hundred feet of the gate, the entire mass of people around us swelled forward suddenly. The people directly behind us bumped into my outstretched feet. Cries echoed off the wall as we moved north. On top of the ramparts many people encouraged the pilgrims forward with lit torches. Others pointed into the distance before us, over the lower and upper parts of Jerusalem.

I turned myself upon the cart. I looked over John's shoulder and saw far off the cause for the general alarm. Perhaps two miles away and covering the entire area beyond the northernmost Valley Gate was a new encampment. More Romans. Thousands upon thousands. Horses. Flags. Fires. The ringing of weapons. Even further to the left, toward the setting sun, I saw large towers rising like black skeletons against the sky.

"Siege towers," I whispered.

"I don't know if I can make it to the gate before they close this side as well," John shouted over his shoulder. He motioned to the nearer gate with his chin. The edge of the road rose, and a spur branched toward the opening. There was no way John could move forward with both the cart and the two of us on for the ride. I tapped Mathias on the arm. He looked at me with wide eyes, a streak of spittle glistening in his gray beard.

"We have to get off!" I shouted.

I had not realized how loud it was around us until I barely heard my own words. But my riding partner understood, all too well, and stumbled off the back of the cart. John, feeling the loss of weight and probably fearing the worse, stopped and looked back. By this time Mathias had reached the front of his small cart and took one handle from John's grasp. My legs were stiff from the long ride but

I forced myself forward. Though the left edge of the road was not smooth, it was also not in the way of so many streaming behind us, so I shifted to the side and dragged myself forward.

Ten minutes later, I lost sight of the cart, and fell well behind John. I pulled myself through the still open gate. Temple guards on both sides screamed for all within range of their voices to hurry through the opening. Others behind them screamed that they were to shut the gate immediately.

After a few moments, I found my breath and straightened to look around. Moving toward me from the shadows just within the gate came John. He blew out a great sigh when his eyes locked on me.

"I saw Anna. She found Miriam and then thought we might be forced to this gate," he said. "The two of them watched us from the top of the Royal portico as we came around the end of the Temple."

John reached out to hold both my shoulders and moved his lips close to my ear.

"Anna said there was fighting off to the west, and in the Upper City. A dozen temple guards and their leaders were caught by a Roman patrol."

My heart went chill. "Abram?"

John shook his head. "No. Abram is fine. He is on the parapet, watching the Romans. I sent Anna and Miriam down below into the stores. They can wait there in safety until the gates reopen."

He came still closer.

"The Sanhedrin is called," he said. "There is talk about crucifixions tonight. The guards the Romans caught. Up on the Skull."

Chapter 14

Crucified

I climbed beside John to the level of the Temple courts, asking any official I found where the Sanhedrin planned to gather this evening. If they were to meet, certainly it should be here, protected by both the high Temple walls and the Lord in heaven. I needed to be there. But no one seemed to know of any plans to gather the leaders.

After I found Anna and Miriam, new and horrifying rumors passed like a fire among those in the Temple. Crosses were being built on Golgotha west of the City. Some said the dozen prisoners taken during the Roman raids would be crucified the upcoming dawn.

John's shoulders slumped at the reports. Then, he stiffened, made a round of curt farewells, and moved off to find his people.

After the moon rose high over the wall to the east, the noise and chaos slipped away. Sometime after midnight, Abram arrived out of the darkness and led us back through the tunnels below the courts. The ceilings were heavily covered with artwork and lit by hundreds of torches and lanterns. The solidness of the Temple was reassuring, as was the so familiar smell of thousands of animals and their food stocks.

We passed through the East Gate and walked back to our village. Despite my misgivings, the Romans had not entered the homes earlier in the day, though we could see the tracks of their steeds on almost every street.

Mid-morning the next day, I left my room to the sound of Anna crying. Seeing me, she calmed herself and tilted a pitcher over my water cup. I reached out to stop her. She had stayed with me these past few years since her husband died. Yet, here I stood, suddenly unsure if I could do anything to truly protect her.

"I am sorry," I said.

Miriam came out of the shadow of her room, rubbing the night out of her eyes. She grinned sadly, her lids dark and heavy, her hair a knotted mess.

"I am sorry," I repeated.

My girls looked at each other. My granddaughter came near and the three of us enveloped each other in a warm embrace.

"Any news?"

Anna released me and turned away. She whispered, "There are crosses. Abram checked on us a while ago. He said the wood can be seen easily from the Temple wall. So far, they are empty."

"Trying to scare us," I said. "They'll wait to carry out their sentences until the city is fully awake."

"There are twelve of them."

"Twelve?"

She nodded.

"They certainly are making a point," Miriam said.

The morning passed in painful silence, broken only when Miriam excused herself to her room. Around mid-day, Anna shuffled into the courtyard and reclined upon a cushion next to the unlit fire. She closed her eyes and her chin soon rested on her chest. I covered her with a thin blanket, but after she slept for an hour, I gently woke her and brought her into her room to nap next to Miriam.

I also went to my room. Try as I might, I could not shake the images of the crosses rising into the sky a couple of miles to the west. What must John think if he saw them now? Eventually, my mind's eye brought before me all the memories of that other crucifixion, the one on the same hill so many years before.

That sad and momentous event began during the night of Passover. I and my family had left our vineyards earlier in the week and came to our small home in Jerusalem. We gathered like all the other Jews in the city to enjoy a meal and recall the events when Moses gained our freedom from Egypt. As the patriarch of our family and leader among my people, I enjoyed the place of honor and proudly told the stories of our faith.

For the preceding week, however, there had been a rising concern within the City. We heard reports that this prophet, Jesus, recovered a man, supposedly from the dead. In between my Passover prayers, I debated these strange happenings with my guests. Many were convinced this man was a great prophet, even though he was barely past thirty years of age and not from our, or any other, school of the Law.

Not me. Since meeting with Jesus, I had come to a decision, though I would never put into words. After witnessing his healing of the leper, I knew he was either the Messiah, or someone serving the devil himself. He could not be only another prophet. He could not be just a teacher; he was either our Christ or he had nothing to offer. I did not need to witness this reported resurrection to understand what was at stake.

I retired to bed, my mind just a bit off due to the evening wine. Before pulling the blankets over me and my wife, I heard many guards march past my home. Much later, I heard the tinkling bells upon soldiers' feet and heard a strange voice among them. Perhaps Galilean, it was hard to hear. Though my room was against the alleyway, the walls and shutters were much more solid in that house than my current home.

Maybe an hour later, in the vague drift of sleep, I heard other marching feet and other voices. Then, a sharp knock on my door. Three Temple guards demanded my presence, even during this most holy of nights. I dressed on the way, being shoved along by tired, and probably half-drunk, guards.

I entered the Sanhedrin and there stood Jesus. His face had been badly beaten and in that very moment I had a sudden and clear realization. This man was, in fact, just that, a man. Therefore, not the Messiah. When he said nothing to counter the high priest's accusations, I was disappointed. When he didn't answer the charges laid against him by even the lowest of our city, I grew impatient. When Jesus finally spoke and essentially said he was the Lord himself, well, I found myself filled with a strange and foreign rage. A few of the others tried to defend him. I joined those shouting down these fools.

Eventually, I realized this night was not going to end simply in this man's humiliation and beating. My colleagues had had enough. Enough stories of miracles and resurrections. Enough with the disorder which did nothing but draw the ire of the Romans. They had devised a story by which they could justify what they had long desired. It was then that Jesus turned, and our eyes met.

His hair was bloody and matted to his forehead. His lip was split high and deep into the corner of his mouth. One eye was nearly closed, but the other stared right at me. And I quivered.

Regardless, I could not move. I barely noticed when the trial culminated in his condemnation. I just stood. Mute. Helpless.

Through my youthful pride, I had once betrayed this man as a baby. Now, through my meekness and silence, I failed him again.

I remained in the shadows as they took him to Herod and then on to Pilate. I waited outside alone and heard the echo of the crowds yelling, 'Crucify him!'

None of the followers of Jesus were seen, certainly none of them were heard. None even came to help carry his burden as he dragged his cross over the dusty streets. I and a few others waited outside the gate. The Skull stood anxiously behind us. The stench of that place surrounded us. There seemed to be not a breath of wind.

I waited until Jesus and the two thieves passed and followed them to the hill. Somewhere during my climb, I noticed my friend Joseph walking beside me. I hadn't seen him for weeks; he must have just returned the night before to celebrate Passover. His home was not far, and he never missed the major feasts in the Holy City. For some reason, we had grown apart these past few months. I never asked him if the rumors of him secretly following the Nazarene were true. I'm not sure if my interactions with Jesus did more to hurt Joseph's reputation or if his rumored faith did more to damage how the other leaders saw me. But here we were, stumping up that terrible hill on a sunny spring morning to watch an unjust death. Unable to even speak to each other.

As we approached, three men were lifted high above us. The

Chief Priest and a couple dozen others stood in a solid line beneath Jesus. To the right cowered maybe five or six women and a young man I thought I might have met before. Below the crosses, Romans soldiers. Enduring what to them was just another long and boring day.

I could not raise my eyes to look at Jesus. As the sun crested the Temple walls, drips fell from his feet, pooling in a sickly bright red splotch upon the ground. I remember a few specks of dirt floating upon his lifeblood and saw the reflection of the white clouds above.

A long pole reached above the heads of the priests. On top, a sponge of sour wine. For some reason, it was that, of all things, which pained me to my core. I shivered and reached out to steady myself against Joseph's shoulder. I turned away as the wine I had drank the night before during Passover soured in my belly. Joseph shook off my hand and turned. I watched him stride purposely down the hill. He removed his head wrap and his fingers interlaced in this hair, pulling. He almost tripped and then he was at the bottom of the hill, melting into the crowd.

I gathered my strength and looked again toward the cross. I felt sick. I turned and bent over, trying not to vomit. My eyes closed. I heard the caw of the birds circling above, the sickening laughter of the Roman guards, the jeering of my colleagues and the cries of those hanging on either side of Jesus. I had a sudden urge to do something, anything. To take even the smallest step to assuage the death of the one I had betrayed.

Instead, I turned and followed Joseph's lead down the hillside. I caught a foot on a rock, lost my sandal and tumbled face first, catching myself with the palms of my hands. Covered in dust, my right fore-toe bleeding, I felt as if every eye outside the city wall stared at me. I hid my face with my hand and rushed on. I entered the upper city with tears stinging my eyes. I wandered the streets, bruising my bare heel until the pain in my foot grew too severe. I then stopped, holding my hand out to steady myself against a wall. I bent over and removed my other sandal. I thought long and hard. What could I do? How could I help?

After a few minutes, I stood and turned to go home. Home to do the only small thing I could think of that could offer anything to the man about to die upon the cross.

I sent my servant, Thomas, with several pieces of gold to the purveyor of spices and herbs. I bathed my sliced foot in water as the afternoon began, wrapped it in fresh linens and sat in silence. The sky turned very dark for a while, which only deepened my mood. I heard a great tumult and people rushing back and forth toward the Temple. My natural instinct was to join them, but I could not. I could not show my face in public. I did not want to show my face to the Lord. At dusk would come the Sabbath and many official duties. That would be more than soon enough for me to come forth.

As the hours passed, I almost willed myself to become sick so as to avoid my upcoming duties. Suddenly, Joseph arrived. He did not dare come to my front gate, so I heard his four quick raps against my window frame.

"Joseph?" I asked. My voice was raw, giving proof of my tears.

Joseph whispered very quietly beyond my window. I went close, moving a stool out of the way.

"I am getting his body," Joseph said.

His body, I thought. The image of Jesus hanging lifeless from the tree, and so quickly, almost knocked me back physically.

I pulled back the shutter and the light outside was painfully bright. Joseph stood before me, picking at a sliver in the window frame. The long, curly hair that usually sprung playfully over his head was matted down and wet. The old gray scar under his left eye which turned up at the edges like a smile appeared raw and angry. I had longed to see him for months but now I could barely raise my eyes to him.

His eyes were rimmed red and his long stare unblinking. The muscles of his jaw ground beneath his beard. As he spoke, I almost had to recoil from the heat of his breath.

"I went to Pilate," he said. His voice carried a trace of the quivering fear he must have felt before the Roman. Joseph no longer served in any capacity as a Jewish leader. As a tradesman, however, he did know some of the Roman language and he had ties with many of the Emperor's functionaries.

"Good," I said. "I have already sent my men to buy embalming oils."

Joseph looked at me with surprise. I don't know why he had come, perhaps simply to find help in moving Jesus' body, but I think he half expected a fight, and certainly not my immediate cooperation.

"I will send Thomas and another servant to help you with the body when they return," I told him.

Joseph nodded. He understood I could not go to the Skull with him, surely the Sanhedrin would keep watch on that horrid place, and the two of us together following the crucifixion might cause concern.

I closed the shutters and left my room. Anna, then in her twenties, helped her mother - my poor Sarah - prepare the meal for this day and the Sabbath, which was almost upon us. Sarah was years from the sickness that would consume her, but she already looked tired.

I called the two of them to me.

"Gather your clothes and prepare to leave. I cannot stay in this city tonight. I cannot stand before the Sanhedrin these next few days. Too dangerous. We must leave. We'll go to my brother's home near the garden before sunset. It's a short ride. After sunrise we will keep to the law but move again out to our vineyard. I will have Simon prepare the horses and a cart. I have an errand to attend to first."

Nightfall was three hours away. I scurried along as fast as my wounded foot would allow, passing through the Upper City. The hour was late. We needed to rush before the Sabbath began.

I mounted an old but reliable donkey kept by the temple guard and rode for about fifteen minutes over uneven ground. To my right rose a small hill with a ridge that fell almost straight down fifteen feet and curved into a stream bed. There, several carved tombs waited for the deaths of their rich and influential owners. The third tomb beyond a short, gnarled tree belonged to Joseph and his family.

I entered the tomb alone, though I could already hear the wheels of a cart creak along the path behind me. I felt a painful desire to hide within this cave from the world beyond. In the small opening,

I found a crate Thomas had filled with the embalming appointments needed to prepare Jesus' body.

"Nicodemus," I heard, "I came as quickly as I could."

Joseph popped his head into the entrance. He ducked and walked down the two small stairs into the tomb. He looked around anxiously and then moved his hand toward the mouth of the cave. A cart backed close to the opening.

"Sorry I'm late," Joseph said, "but his mother, Mary. She was there with the body and I didn't want to rush her. His young disciple eventually eased her away and down the hill. I told him where we were going to bury Jesus."

Joseph spoke far more quickly than I ever heard him speak. He was a businessman, a leader in the political world in Jerusalem and beyond. He had always held himself as a proper Jewish Pharisee in his personal life, the perfect follower of the Lord when dealing with the Romans. In all things, he was a calm and reasoned man. Until these past two years or so. Until he came back from his travels in Galilee with stories of this strange new prophet.

The strangeness that shadowed our recent relationship melted into a tight embrace. He patted me hard on the shoulders and pushed himself away, saying, 'We must be quick'.

"Some of the Temple guards marched toward the Skull as I rode here," I said. "I don't know their plans, but I imagine the Pharisees will not want to take any chances with Jesus' body. We heard the accusations during the trial. We all know what Jesus said about coming back to life, and we know what we read in Scripture.

"Nicodemus," Joseph sighed. "I don't know."

"Don't know what?"

His brows squeezed tight over his face. His eyes shifted this way and that, then settled over my shoulder, looking at the mouth of the cave.

"I don't know what to think now that he's dead. How could this happen? The priests will probably try to destroy his body or burn it. They'd have to do it publicly. And before sundown. We must hurry and roll the stone in front of the cave. Seal Jesus in here and protect his body."

I nodded agreement and opened the crate my servants had

brought. I stared into the box for a moment, stunned. Inside was a massive container of Myrrh and another of aloes. There must have been fifty pounds in the box, maybe seventy, maybe even one hundred! I had given Thomas more than enough to buy what we needed for Jesus. In his rush, he had spent every last lepton.

"Well," I sighed.

I looked at Joseph. For the first time in who knows how long, I smiled. He smiled back loosely and moved back toward the entrance of the tomb.

"Bring him here," he said.

Joseph's man, Annius, stepped down into the cave and two others eased Jesus' linen wrapped body into the tomb from above. We brought him slowly to a stone slab close to the back of the cave. The light outside already grew dim, and Annius held aloft a pair of lit torches. Joseph and I unwrapped the cloths from Jesus slowly, carefully. I had seen many crucifixions under the Roman rule, but for some reason the dark dried blood around the holes in his hands and his feet made my skin tingle.

I moved to the back corner of the slab, across from Joseph. We each held the unwrapped body from under a shoulder, his servants holding the legs from behind the knees and calves. As we moved him onto clean linens, his weight grew quickly given what seemed to be a lean frame. We then uncovered his face and hurriedly unwrapped the rest of his body. I looked at the old set of linens. There was only a smudge or two of blood upon them, almost as if all the blood had been lost already.

I looked back time and again at his hands, his feet, a bloody slice into his side. I could not look toward his face. Even though his head was now covered, I felt as if he stared at me through the shroud.

I mixed the embalming powders with a few hins of water brought by Joseph's men. The myrrh quickly filled the cave with the scent of a dark mint herb. For years after, I could not handle any mint in my home, despite the protests of Sarah and Anna. The remaining powders and aloes I gave to Joseph's servants.

Joseph unwrapped his head scarf. He leaned upon his fists pressed flat upon the burial stone. He stood very still for many minutes, even after my work with the spices was complete. His body shielded my view of Jesus' face as he stared down at the man he had secretly followed for many months.

He grunted suddenly and turned. He stumbled toward the bottom of the stairs, then pressed himself up to the mouth of the cave and into the stale afternoon air.

I turned to his servant and shook my head. I looked down at Jesus' body.

It was a gray color, almost a match with the burial stone. His hands laid flat on the stone, black holes staring up at me. My eyes moved slowly from his legs to his shoulders, grimacing at the large strips of scourged flesh hanging loose. Here and there, I saw the white of bone or sinew.

"I betrayed you once. Today, I failed you again."

I continued to prepare his body. My thoughts grew anxious as I sensed the sun setting to the west. The Sabbath was almost upon us.

Joseph returned a few minutes later, his eyes ringed with red. His breath was sour.

"We must hurry," he said. He reached past me and re-wrapped Jesus' body. "I have a couple other men outside now, to help us with the stone. They brought strange and troubling news. Something happened today in the Temple."

He said the curtain had been torn, words that would have previously made me rush immediately to the Lord's house. But now, the thought of that place meant nothing. My mind was blank. My sight dimmed with the dying day. My breaths became almost too heavy to pull into my chest.

"We can do no more," Joseph said. He called for his men to take the remaining spices away. One of them whispered to Joseph urgently. "The priests are coming, or the Romans. My men see smoke of several torches, but they are not sure. We need to go, now!"

"Go where?" I muttered.

"To our homes," Joseph muttered. "We can meet tomorrow and discuss what next to do. Caiaphas and the others have the blood lust, as do the Romans. We must be careful. We must do what we can to keep the people together and the city at peace. No one will work tomorrow and so there will be too much time to reflect upon strange and dangerous thoughts."

I stood and stared at Joseph. Joseph's shadow now danced on the walls of the tomb before the torch light.

"I cannot," I said. "I will gather my family and leave for my vineyards. I cannot remain around such evil. I must find somewhere to think, Joseph. Will you not come with me?"

Joseph smiled. He patted my shoulder with his thick hand. "Time enough to discuss that later. Let us seal the tomb and leave him in peace. He is in the hands of the Lord now."

Chapter 15

The Cloud

The thought and memories of the Nazarene's decades-old crucifixion remained with me through the mid of the following day. A soft tapping on my window shutters startled me upright. For a moment, I thought for sure that my old friend, Joseph, had come to me again. I opened the window slowly, shading my eyes from the late afternoon sun with my hand. I heard John's voice, this time, whisper for me from around the corner.

"Rabbi, are you alright? And Anna, and Miriam?"

I cleared my throat. "Yes, I believe so. They are napping in their room. We'll have Sabbath prayer and meal later."

"Good," John said. "No one answered your front door. I didn't dare stand in the lane for very long."

"Please, please, come around again, I will open the door right away."

I hurried from my room and opened the front door. John slipped in, hiding his face in the shadows of his brown hood. He turned and bolted shut the door.

"They are not going to wait until tomorrow."

"Who's not going to wait?"

John took a deep breath.

"The Romans," he said. "I heard they are going to wait until after the Sabbath is done, at sunset, and then fill their crosses for all to see."

I shuddered. I backed away from John as if he had slapped me. I stepped toward the door, now not quite ready to invite John into

119

our home.

"John," I said, "I have told you much these past few weeks. I hope what we have discussed helps you in your task."

"It will, rabbi," John said quickly. "Hearing about Jesus from you has reminded me of so much. I see his face in a way I haven't thought about for a long time. I received a letter yesterday, a letter that has both encouraged me to write my story, and also made me even more afraid that I will fail in the task. I don't yet know exactly what to write, but you have helped me greatly. And I have spent long hours in prayer as you suggested."

"Can I then ask you a favor?" I glanced behind John and listened for any sound in the lane beyond our door. I hadn't been able to fully calm myself since we were forced into the Temple the night before. John, standing just paces away from my sleeping girls, was a danger. There was no choice. He had to stay away from my family. At least until after the Passover later this week.

John looked at me steadily, then the corners of his mouth raised into a sad grin. He nodded.

"Of course, rabbi," he said. He took a step back toward the door, his hands rising to the edges of his hood. "You don't need to ask. I understand."

Anna then walked from her room to my side. She looked at me quizzically and asked John to come in and sit.

"Will you join us for dinner?"

"No," John said, still looking at me. "There were dozens of my people killed yesterday when the Romans swept around the city. I am probably not safe being here. Safe for you."

Anna brushed past me and reached for John's arm.

"I insist. It is the Sabbath. Have you not been a Jew for so long that you forget your manners? It will be good for you, and for all of us, to share this special meal. Miriam will enjoy your company."

I stood frozen. John looked at me and tilted his head.

I breathed deep, then nodded.

Anna led the two of us to the courtyard as she tied on her scarlet apron. She motioned to a pair of chairs, muttering about keeping us out of her way in the kitchen. She bent over to set a fire in the pit and shooed John away when he offered to help.

"I didn't hear of any deaths," I said as I sat. "Though I assumed many had been injured last night."

"The Sanhedrin sent their guards out to clear the streets of the bodies, both alive and dead. They didn't even light torches to see who the people were."

"Makes sense, I suppose. They want nothing to deter the pilgrims from coming to the Temple for Passover."

"I think my people fell under the blades of the Temple guard and not the Romans."

"Well," Anna said firmly. "You have nothing to fear here. Abram made it clear to his fellow guards, they are not to bother my father again."

"It's not just the guards...."

"Hush!" Anna said. "You are no safer out there than here with us. You will stay with us for our Sabbath meal, and may the Lord we all serve protect us, and all the people of the city, from ourselves and these Roman invaders."

John relented. Soon, he and I were deep in discussion around a fire in the courtyard. I told John about the day Jesus died, the hours after he and Mary had been forced away from his body by the Roman guards. John confirmed that Joseph came to a few of the disciples that evening. He told them Jesus was buried and if the tomb was not guarded the next morning, following the Sabbath, he would send men to help move the stone away if they wanted to better prepare the body.

"Who did he think would guard it?" I asked.

"Temple guards. The Romans," John shrugged. "Didn't you know the other Jewish leaders asked Pilate to post a Roman guard. To make sure we didn't steal the body, I would think."

"No," I said. "I was so angry with what happened I left that very Sabbath eve. I never heard that. Things were never again the same between me and the others in the Sanhedrin."

"No, they certainly were not," John said. "When Jesus was alive and teaching us, we thought we knew what we were being called to do. Then he died. Then he returned and the Spirit came. Everything changed. After the Spirit came, one of us was brought before the Sanhedrin. Stephen. He was stoned."

"Yes," I said. "I remember. There was another young man there, you knew him well. He was quite angry and passionate then. Some of us warned him to treat your people as fellow Jews, to let things work out as God intended. Even though I was his elder, I didn't have the courage to speak out against him or the others who wanted your friend murdered."

John, surprisingly, laughed. He nodded vigorously.

"Ahhh, yes. Paul possessed a special kind of zeal, did he not?"

I nodded. "He would not allow Stephen to be spared and after your friend's very interesting sermon to us, most of the elders were all too willing to go along with Saul."

"Well," John said, "we knew what Jesus had taught us. We felt the compulsion of the Spirit to preach the good news to everyone. We understood the need to leave the Holy City and go throughout the world. And yet we hesitated. We thought, perhaps, that we would eventually convince you and the others in the Sanhedrin, and together our people would rise up to bring word of the Christ to the world."

John paused. His eyes held steady into the dark gray sky above my courtyard.

"I came before you once," he said. "Before the Sanhedrin. I don't know if you were there, or if you would even remember me. Peter and I had been arrested by the Temple guard. We both thought that this was the moment."

"The moment...?"

John turned to me with a rush. "This was the moment we'd tell you of the risen Messiah and you would join us to bring the Kingdom of God to the world."

John shrank back and sighed. He looked at his hands in his lap.

"Sorry. We were not ready. We stumbled before you, thinking we were surely about to die. But we thought God would give us the perfect words to convince all of you to take up the Lord's cause. We did not understand the resistance of the leaders. We had seen our Lord come back from the dead, how could anyone not understand? How could the rest of the Chosen People not understand? Well, we left still breathing and encouraged by God's protection. But, we finally realized, right then and there. You would not join us. The

Jewish people would not be the tool God would use to bring his good news to the world. Our call was clear. We followed it. Me to Ephesus. The others throughout the world."

John looked at me without wavering.

"We had to go. We had to leave our people behind."

A million images flooded my mind in a moment. So many meetings, so many arguments. Saul leading us against these Christ followers, and then abandoning us. Word that the Galilean's followers soon gathered seemingly in every land of the empire. Even in Rome itself. And we, the leaders of the people, the Chosen People of God, turning in upon ourselves. Seeing all our hope in the Temple alone. Feeling vindicated these past few years by our expulsion of the Romans.

"Dinner is almost ready," Miriam called.

John and I looked at each other for a long moment. We both began to speak at once. John laughed and deferred with a smile.

"I am afraid for you," I said.

"Me?"

"Yes. I have thought a lot about your friend Jesus. About his death. Now we have crosses rising in the hills to the west. I know the Romans blame your people for the fire in Rome. You should consider leaving the city altogether. At least until after the Passover. Besides, I'm not sure how much more I can tell you about Jesus."

John chuckled. Then, his eyes turned serious and he raised his eyebrows.

"Nicodemus," he said. "I appreciate that. The Romans are out there, but they certainly have not traveled all this way with all these men to search for a few of us who follow Christ. There are many other cities easier for them to search for us. If they wanted to hang my people from those trees, they would have just come here with a small garrison and enough gold to pay your Sanhedrin to turn us over."

My jaw clenched. Despite the fire, I shook with a sudden chill.

Of course, I thought. *Of course, he is right.*

Miriam walked into the courtyard and broke the sudden shadow of my fears. She held out her hand.

"Come, grandfather," she said. "Lead us in our Sabbath meal."

"In a moment, dear," I said. I smiled at Miriam and she went back to Anna.

I leaned toward John.

"Perhaps you are right. For one of us or the other, our time may be short. Teach me. I don't mean I want you to convert me to believing in your Christ. I am far too old a man for that. I just want to understand. I want to know what my granddaughter finds so interesting about your ways. I want to know why the Saul I knew left his people. And what did Stephen die for? And your other friends? Remember, you also promised me an answer to the questions I still have from that night I met your Jesus."

John pressed his lips together. He reached up and rubbed the end of his short beard within his fingers. He then looked up to the sky and grinned for a long moment.

"I can't necessarily tell you," he said. "But tomorrow. Tomorrow, I can show you if you are willing."

Chapter 16

Gathering

The night following Sabbath passed without incident. The crosses stood aloft, and empty, upon Golgotha the next morning. The rumors of overnight terrors had not come true. Perhaps, I thought, with Passover now only a few days away, the Romans might still be reasonable. I had often been an emissary to them in the past, perhaps I could help my people in this way again.

I had slept well once the urgent fear of the executions faded. But, yet again, I woke before the dawn. The cloudless morning was bright. I dressed slowly and went to our table. John had slept on a mat the previous night, but he was also already dressed and slowly sipping water from a wooden cup. My girls moved about sleepily. Miriam bumped into Anna and my daughter swatted her in the rear with a laugh.

John cleared his throat and reached into his cloak. He pulled out a small scroll. He held it out to me should I be interested.

"From who?" I asked.

He smiled broadly as Miriam snatched the scroll from his hand. I taught my granddaughter to read both Greek and Hebrew many years before. I was often saddened by how much of my library was sold over the years when need arose.

"I didn't want to interrupt the Sabbath for you with this," John said, gently pulling the scroll back from Miriam's hand. "This is one of the scrolls from a letter recently received from Paul."

Miriam's hand dropped to her side. Her other hand rose to cover her mouth.

"Paul?" she muttered excitedly. She turned her head to look at me.

I held her gaze and my face warmed. Hadn't there been enough talk of Saul the night before?

"I am sorry," John said. He held the scroll before his face. "Reading this was like hearing again from a long-lost friend. It arrived two days ago. Rabbi, this letter has taught me much in terms of what and how I must write about the Lord. Anyway, as you know, today is our day of celebration. I have been asked to read part of this to a gathering of believers here in Jerusalem. If you will grant me the honor, I invite you all to attend, should you wish."

Anna stood, brushed clean her clothing and retired into her room without a word. I began to stand as well. John had been a pleasure to know since his arrival, but this - especially in what may soon be a time of great need for our people - this was taking things a step too far. And yet.... I walked over to Miriam. I know she wanted to go with John, and something told me I wouldn't be able to stop her if I tried. And I would not her risk going alone. The Romans certainly have no love for John's people.

"We'll go with you," I said.

"Good," John smiled. "I am honored. And perhaps, father Nicodemus, I can show you something at our gathering that might help answer the questions troubling you for so long."

There were a number of cart-runners in the city to help the mass of pilgrims arrived for Passover. John hired one to pull us around the southern tip of the Temple, crossing the road to Bethlehem, and back up to the upper city. There, we entered a nondescript home. Two very small swerving lines were etched into the wood of the outer door. I had seen this mark more and more often since we ejected the Romans from the Holy City. Once the door was closed behind us - the windowless room turned dark. My eyes ached, gasping for light. John stood still by me. Miriam moved toward him. We were all three breathless.

There was then a noise, seemingly from below us, followed by the sound of thumping against wood. The lit outline of a rectangular shape appeared beneath us and then a lid of some sort scratched out of the way. A man's head popped up through the opening. He looked at us, then lifted a small torch above the level of the floor.

His eyes smiled and his mouth widened into a joyous laugh.

"John!" he cried. He caught himself and snapped his mouth shut. I felt as if the entire city must have heard his shout. But the sounds of the outer world, muffled by the thick, closed door, continued on as before.

"Polis, my friend," John said. He motioned to Miriam and me to move toward the mouth of what was obviously the entrance to a tunnel.

"I am sorry," he said. "We go through these tunnels to our places of worship to protect us. They requested you also go below to protect the location of their church."

Miriam virtually jumped into the hole. As I eased closer, I noticed steps, carved into the dirt, receding into a low tunnel. Miriam had already been led away from the mouth and I only caught a glimpse of the back of her flowing robe.

"I will help you," John whispered to me.

"I don't know if I like Miriam being here," I said.

"She is perfectly safe," John assured me. His strong hand took hold of my upper arm and he led me down onto the first step.

"That is not what I am afraid of," I whispered.

John looked at me for a moment and half crouched to stand at my height as we moved under the Jerusalem world.

The two of us had finally come to the point of decision, and we both understood. I was willing to help him find some memory to aide his writing. Perhaps he and his people would come to know through my memories something about how their young Galilean rabbi fit, and didn't fit, within our Jewish world. And perhaps John could even teach me something I could never quite piece together on my own. What did Jesus mean that night when he seemed to say the spirit of God could go to the Gentiles if it wished?

But Miriam? Here? At this event where people call upon God, call upon my God, for blessings through a man I helped bury? A man they believe is no longer dead? A man I betrayed and then failed?

I could not leave Miriam here alone. That I knew. Suddenly, I felt an overwhelming rage. Surely, John had sent Miriam into the tunnel before me as a trap! He knew I would not abandon her.

A moment or two passed as I stared at the dirt floor. I then turned to look at John. He only nodded with a soft smile. His grip of my arm eased, and he moved his hand upon my shoulder, then to the back of my neck.

"Rabbi Nicodemus," he said gently.

In that moment, I knew there had been no centrifuge. He had not tricked me. He was not here with any undue expectations.

"I just want you to understand us better," he whispered.

I turned toward him.

"I know. But I am an old man. John, I have betrayed my faith and my God before. I don't know how I feel about any of this."

John escorted me down the tunnel. It was cramped and smelled like the turned fields in our vineyard after a heavy rain. I only needed to nod my head, but John had to bend over several times. Twice, he had to let me go on ahead when the tunnel narrowed. To the right, we passed a small room with many long holes carved into the walls. Bundles of white cloth filled several of the openings. In another place, there was an ornate wooden chest set upon a small table. The lid was open, and I could see a few scrolls within.

After maybe a hundred winding steps, another chiseled set of stairs rose from the bottom of the tunnel. Above, another wooden lid or hatch of some kind. We had already passed two other such lids, two other similar sets of stairs. Our guide, Polis, walked up the stairs and through the opening into a large, dark room above. I briefly saw the back of Miriam's blue dress as she had already moved up out of the tunnel. I sighed deeply. John again patted me gently on the shoulder.

"Please," he said, "I had them place comfortable cushions in the back, a bit out of sight. I mean no disrespect, but I think it will help the others feel more comfortable."

We rose out of the tunnel and into a large room. I walked slowly to my place. I caught Miriam's smile for a moment as she also sat. There were two long tables toward what seemed to be the front of the room. Upon one was a wide bowl of clear liquid, perhaps water. On the second was a tray of bread and several pitchers.

Before the tables, several hundred people sat quietly. Men and women gathered together, perhaps by family. A few children sat here and there. One pair of young brothers sat off to my right, pushing each other in the shadows and earning a swat from their father. To the far right, perhaps twenty people stood, wearing white linens around their shoulders.

All of the people were silent and now watched John walk to the front of the room. He met another man there with a wide smile. They embraced and then the other man, obviously a leader of some sort within this community, sat upon a cushion in front of the long tables.

John turned and said, "You have all greeted me these past few weeks with the grace and warmth of our Lord. May his peace be with you all."

The crowd responded in turn. I did not notice whether Miriam said anything.

"I know," John continued, "that we are all troubled by what is happening outside these walls. The return of the Romans. But," he paused, looking left to right across those gathered, "we know that the Lord is in control and he will protect us should that be his will. As I have reminded you these past weeks, heed the words of Christ that we have passed along to you. We lived with our Lord and walked with him in these very streets. Our words are true."

There was a quiet murmur, many before me nodded to each other.

"Now," John said. His smile returned. "I know we have much to do this day. Next week we remember the death and resurrection. That most holy event."

"Holy?" I whispered. *That horrible day on the cross?*

"Today, however," John said, looking at the leaders sitting before him, "we also continue with the sacred duty of teaching and bringing new believers into the body."

He looked to his left at those dressed in white. "While you are not yet fully part of us, we give God thanks for your presence. Before we continue, I would like all of us to hear the words of Paul, our beloved brother who was killed in Rome doing the work of the Lord. I have received a letter. Perhaps it is the last he wrote. It was addressed to the church in the very city that took his life."

He stopped and looked down at the scroll he held before him. Long moments passed. I wondered if any of the people here actually once knew Saul.

"Since we have people about to join us, from many backgrounds and many cultures, I would like to read just the part of his words that seem most appropriate. For the Lord has brought all of us the opportunity to believe and to be redeemed for eternal life."

He unrolled part of the scroll and held it up. Since all of the windows had been covered to protect the privacy of this gathering, he moved before a large lamp. His voice deepened as he read to make it easy for all to hear.

"In Rome," he began, "Paul was concerned about our brothers and sisters trying to live together, some Jew, some Gentile. He writes correctly when he tells us that we all need the saving work of Jesus. Paul wrote the following:

> *For not all who are descended from Israel are Israel. Nor because they are his descendants are they all Abraham's children.*
>
> *In other words, it is not the children by physical descent who are God's children, but it is the children of the promise who are regarded as Abraham's offspring. For this was how the promise was stated: "At the appointed time I will return, and Sarah will have a son."*
>
> *Not only that, but Rebekah's children were conceived at the same time by our father Isaac. Yet, before the twins were born or had done anything good or bad-- in order that God's purpose in election might stand: not by works but by him who calls--she was told, "The older will serve the younger." Just as it is written: "Jacob I loved, but Esau I hated."*

> *What then shall we say? Is God unjust?*
> *Not at all! For he says to Moses,*
> *"I will have mercy on whom I have*
> *mercy, and I will have compassion on*
> *whom I have compassion."*
> *It does not, therefore, depend on*
> *human desire or effort, but on God's*
> *mercy.*

John stopped, then held the parchment higher and began again from the beginning. I am sure many around me did not have the training and understanding I developed through decades of study. But I knew what Saul was writing about. He had learned the Holy Scriptures as I had.

Jacob? I thought. Esau? The Jews and the Gentiles. Did Saul really have the nerve to write that God's blessings upon Abraham does not belong to all those descended of Israel? That some of the Gentiles, the cursed descendants of Esau, would also now receive the same blessing through faith in this Christ?

I stood and backed into the shadows of the room.

My people have sacrificed for centuries to obey every word of the Lord, I thought. We study and sacrifice and praise and tithe. And yet Saul thought that despite all this, not all of us are due the blessings of God? How can this be? Don't we follow a just and righteous Lord?

John finished. The gathering pondered silently. John rolled out the scroll, found another part he wanted to read, and then looked up. He coughed to clear his throat.

"Later in his letter, Paul wrote:

> *Again I ask: Did the Jews stumble so as to*
> *fall beyond recovery? Not at all! Rather,*
> *because of their transgression, salvation*
> *has come to the Gentiles to make Israel*
> *envious. But if their transgression means*
> *riches for the world, and their loss means*

131

riches for the Gentiles, how much greater riches will their full inclusion bring!

I am talking to you Gentiles. Inasmuch as I am the apostle to the Gentiles, I take pride in my ministry in the hope that I may somehow arouse my own people to envy and save some of them. For if their rejection brought reconciliation to the world, what will their acceptance be but life from the dead? If the part of the dough offered as first fruits is holy, then the whole batch is holy; if the root is holy, so are the branches.

If some of the branches have been broken off, and you, though a wild olive shoot, have been grafted in among the others and now share in the nourishing sap from the olive root, do not consider yourself to be superior to those other branches. If you do, consider this: You do not support the root, but the root supports you. You will say then, "Branches were broken off so that I could be grafted in." Granted. But they were broken off because of unbelief, and you stand by faith. Do not be arrogant, but tremble. For if God did not spare the natural branches, he will not spare you either."

John stopped and looked to his left. He held the scroll before those who were obviously being trained for initiation into this community.

"You yourselves come to us from many backgrounds. Know that we all share a place at the Lord's table. We all rely upon him for the forgiveness of our sins. Not one of you, not one of us, is better than any other."

I shook my head, my mouth dropped open. I looked to my left

and quickly found the door I had entered through. I stumbled through the shadows toward that exit. In the anteroom, I found the opening to the tunnel and quickly descended. It was dark, so I removed the torch hanging on the wall. I started off in the direction from which we came and lost myself in thought beneath the streets of the Holy City.

I could understand, perhaps, that not all those of Jacob are truly the descendants of Abraham in spirit. As much as any I knew of my own weaknesses and sins. But now Saul claimed that those of Esau - Gentiles we would not even eat with lest we become unclean! - he now claimed they were also called by God and could become true sons of whatever promise was to come through their Christ? Of course, there were some Gentiles who come to believe in the living God and agree to follow our ways. But where is it written that they could simply join with us and do whatever they please in following this so-called Christ?

My sad prayer echoed in the dark as I stumbled through the tunnels:

> *He who dwells in the shelter of the Most High will rest in the shadow of the Almighty. I will say of the Lord, 'He is my refuge and my fortress, my God, in whom I trust.'*

Chapter 17

Rejection

The following four days were an unending storm, growing ever angrier. John may be a fisherman, but not me. I do not like the feel of the very ground beneath my feet swell up and down, giving way all around.

I do not like the sense of impending failure, especially when it comes to the two tasks my old body has been given. Keeping my children safe and protecting the people of God.

After escaping John's gathering, I felt chilled, as if facing a fever. Two hours later, I walked into our home alone and faced the angry gaze of Anna. I stiffened against a scolding. For taking Miriam to John's people. Even more for not bringing her back. But, perhaps, my daughter was satisfied with my downcast eyes. Perhaps I looked as bad as I felt. I staggered to my room and collapsed onto my bed.

Those people! John! Miriam! With Gentiles? What nonsense was this?

I rolled over and caught myself whispering, 'Blessed be he who opens the eyes of the blind."

My old mind rolled over and over upon John and his Jesus. Had he healed the possessed? Did he really give sight to the blind? Could he have raised Lazarus from the dead?

"Grant me insight."

I could not shove aside the image of Jesus on the hill beside the sea the day I witnessed his healing touch for myself. He had cleansed a leper! He had!

But then I thought about those wretched Romans standing

beneath his cross. How many crucifixions had I seen before his? And yet, for the first time, for the very first time, I noticed the heels. Jesus' feet had been stripped bare of skin as he stumbled under the weight of the tree, carrying the instrument of his own torture. Now, those heels were pressed against, and nailed into, a small board holding up his feet. He had to press up against those exposed bones just to gasp a breath.

Why was that the thing which made me turn away and race down the hillside?

I stood up for this Nazarene several times, trying to make up for my betrayal when he was a babe. But that Friday morning as I stood behind my Jewish brothers, staring up at the Cross, I understood I now stood apart from the others. In some way, forever apart from the leaders of my people.

Before I started down the hillside, as if God had spoken the words directly into my ears, I heard the words of Genesis, "He will crush your head and you will strike his heel."

Who would strike his heel? I thought. The devil? And yet here we were. Us. We were the ones striking his heels as he hung above us.

I turned from this would-be King of the Jews. I was desperately angry as I stormed down that hillside. How could this man shake the foundation of my beliefs, give me such a glimmer of hope? Hang from that cross as if a common criminal? Then cry out, "Forgive them, they know not what they do?'

Forgive us? As if he had no shame upon that tree left for himself! He hung naked as Adam before his fall, and he had left me and all of us who were dressed as the most honored of our people....he left us in shame. He was willing to forgive since we knew not what we were doing. Would he also forgive what I did to the children of Bethlehem? I knew not what I was doing then!

"Please, please," I said to the dark ceiling of my room, 'grant me sight. Help me to see."

I closed my eyes and again imagined the new Roman crosses. This time, they stood empty and threatening just a few miles away. There were not three crosses now, but twelve. Not surrounded by a few bored guards but by entire legions of Roman soldiers threatening battle.

But what could I do? I am an old man. I hadn't attended the Sanhedrin for more than, what, a decade? Like John, I was all alone. Those I served with had passed on years before. Only I had been left alive.

Only I had been left to help my people.

I pushed myself up from my bed and walked to my chest. I opened it and threw back blankets and cloaks and various garments. There, near the bottom, was the mantle that once signified my position. Heavily tasseled but now frayed with age. I pulled it on and reached, slowly and carefully, for my me'il. The cloth passed now beyond my knees, the long sleeves draped around my arms. I felt like a child in man's clothing.

I hoped my man's clothing would impress the children now running the Sanhedrin. Certainly, they would remember all I had done for God's people. The lower levels of the Temple itself were decorated by workman I paid for. Certainly, these new leaders would honor the friend and teacher of their fathers and honor me with one last opportunity to speak with the Romans on the behalf of God's people. I lacked the wild passions of their youth and perhaps that alone might provide what was needed to make my effort a success.

I entered the outer room deep in thought. Anna was in the central courtyard, tending a fire before preparing dinner. She saw me and walked into our home. Suddenly, I realized what she was about to see, and she would realize what I was planning to do. I turned to hurry toward the door.

"You took our daughter to John's people," she said. "You turned your back on our God. Why are you dressed like that now? You are going to break the rules and go to the Sanhedrin? You are no longer welcomed there."

Clearly, she had been planning her argument throughout the morning. But I was doing this for her. To keep the Roman army away. Did she not realize that?

But Anna's scolding never came. As I stood dumbfounded, she called through the window to the young boy, Matthew, who lived next door. She asked him to find Josiah, a friend and fellow guard with Abram. Josiah peeked his head in through the window a few minutes later, his cheek dusted with the flour he used to crust his well-loved pies. He looked at my clothing and smiled broadly.

"Go to the Temple," Anna told him, "and find someone who can bring father before the Sanhedrin."

Josiah rushed off without a question. As we waited, Anna pulled and pinched my clothing, smiled into my face like a little child, and then walked with me toward the East Gate.

I was more than winded when we arrived. I welcomed the cool shadows beside the Temple walls. We found Josiah quickly enough and he helped me along the short flights of stairs leading up to the Court of the Gentiles. We walked through the chaos of dozens of stands now set up to sell any number of goods needed by the pilgrims arriving for Passover. We continued into the Court of the Women. I paused before continuing toward the inner courts. I did not welcome the idea of leaving Anna in the court all by herself.

I need not have worried. Several of the younger members of the Sanhedrin came toward us with Josiah. They marched close and moved Anna and me away from the middle of the court and toward the eastern edge.

"What is it you want, old man?" the middle of the three men said. I knew his face but could not at first bring forward his name. Jude! Yes, Jude, son of Simon.

"I have come to help," I said. The three men looked at each other and grunted.

"We don't have time for this," the one on the right said. "The Romans surround our Holy Temple...."

"Exactly," I interrupted. I held my arms out.

"Exactly what?" they asked.

"All of you were part of the uprising," I said. "The Romans know that. They will not deal with you."

"Really," Jude said. "Are you so sure? We have pulled together quite the horde of gold and silver. They will certainly listen to that."

"Are you so confident in your little treasure?"

We all fell silent for a moment. Anna stepped forward, pulled herself as tall as she could and spoke first.

"The Romans are not here for gold. What could you offer that

Caesar cannot?"

The three men stared at Anna, then turned toward me. Jude shook his head angrily.

"Perhaps not. And, perhaps you do still have friends among the Romans. We all remember quite well what you have done for them, Rabbi."

The man to the right stepped forward. "Or perhaps you want to find your old friend Herod and cut a deal with him again. You may have bought your seat on the Sanhedrin, but we remember the stories of our fathers. We know what you did in Bethlehem. Even if we thought the Romans would talk to you, why would we think you would speak for us and not for them?"

Jude pulled his friend back by the shoulder.

"Enough," Jude said. "Listen, we don't have any time for this. Perhaps we should just let you go out to them. Perhaps they have a cross up on the Skull that would be small enough even for you."

Anna began to push past me. I held my hand out to stop her. Jude ignored her and continued.

"Besides, you will soon have plenty of friends hanging with you. The Romans marched here for the Christ followers. And perhaps your new friends hanging on those crosses will be enough to satisfy them. We certainly don't need you to negotiate for us, Rabbi. They will listen to the gold and they will be satisfied with the blood of those who burned their capital city."

I looked over the heads of the three men toward the Holy of Holies. How could God allow men of such stupidity protect his holy Temple?

"They are not here for those who follow Jesus," I said. "Are you that blind? I knew your fathers. I was friends with them. I know they raised you smarter than this. If the Romans came here for the Christ followers, would they have brought several legions? They would not have come here seeking gold, but instead to give you gold so you would turn over the followers of Jesus, if that was their goal. How can you be so blind? They are here, with this force, to destroy us and this Temple. That is why you need me."

Jude's hands squeezed into tight fists. Our guide, Josiah, looked down at the stone pavers.

"Our fathers were never your friends," Jude said. "We know how you became so wealthy and we know you gave only blood money back to this Holy Place. You are a disgrace. Go back to your bed where you belong. We will take care of the Romans."

With that, the three men turned and marched off. Josiah paused as if he was going to walk us back to our home, and then he turned to follow the three Pharisees, marching a few steps behind. I watched until they entered the Holy Place. I couldn't breathe. My cloak's weight felt overbearing on my back and neck.

Anna touched my shoulder. She turned me around and we walked toward the Court of the Gentiles together.

"Blood money!" I gasped. "I never...."

Anna stopped up short. I turned toward her. Her eyes were full of tears.

"Don't you listen to them," she said. "I don't care what they say. I have heard it all before."

"You have?" I asked. The blood drained from my face.

"The women used to talk like this," my daughter said.

"I had no idea. You stayed here with me in the city and had to listen to all this?"

Anna grabbed me by the hand and marched me toward the outer court. She sniffled once or twice but when I looked at her, her head was erect. She smiled pleasantly at all those we passed.

"I am the daughter of the beloved Rabbi Nicodemus."

I stumbled along, leaving the Holy Temple for the last time.

Chapter 18

Debate

Anna shouted at someone outside my door.

"He doesn't understand!"

I had been drifting in and out of sleep since we returned from the Temple. The din in the streets was no longer the constant hum of a great city preparing for the celebration. Instead, bands of scurrying feet passed by my home, first in one direction, then the other. Twice, the rhythmic crunch of armored soldiers grew and fell, punctuated by the whinnying of battle horses. Still, without pause it seemed, the slow march of sacrificial animals continued, just at the edge of my hearing. I could picture the animals and their tenders filling the lower levels of the Temple.

John's voice broke into my thoughts.

"He came up with the idea of going to the Sanhedrin all on his own? Don't you know how dangerous it is for him out there?"

"Don't you dare...," Anna started. I heard her fists slam against the top of our table. "I am sorry, but you have also brought danger into our home. I have worked too long and hard to keep my father out of sight and quiet. He can barely stand some days, much less defend himself."

I pushed the cover down my bed. I smacked my thighs, trying to warm my legs. After a few moments, I forced myself to an elbow, then swung my legs, one after the other, over the edge of my bed. I was soon sitting in the dimness, the candles in the outer room twinkling around my door frame.

"No one knows I come here," John said.

"Oh!" Anna gasped. "I've been out there, out there in that city. I keep my mouth shut, and I hear everything. Even the young Pharisees talked about my father's 'new friends'."

I pushed myself to my feet, standing still for a long moment to make sure I would not topple over. I edged toward the door, leaning with one elbow against its frame.

"Do you not know what happened in Rome?"

John sighed heavily. "Of course, I do. I live in Ephesus, information travels quite quickly there. Many of my friends died in Rome."

"Sorry, I didn't mean to offend you," Anna said. "I don't understand you, but I know you are an honorable man. I am sorry for your losses. But there is confusion everywhere. Those Romans you hear marching by. Another band heading for the Fort of Antonia. I've been watching from the roof. They are part of more than one army gathering out there. Since we forced them out of the city, they come back occasionally with just enough force to scare our leaders into submitting to some demand or another. But now entire legions are gathering. Yes, I know it was dangerous to bring my father to the Temple, but I thought maybe he was right. These infants don't know how to deal with the Romans. Maybe he can!"

"Why?" John asked. "Do you know why the Romans are here?"

"Jesus," my daughter said simply.

John snorted.

"I am sorry," he said. "But to the Romans, my Lord is just one more person they nailed to a cross. And Jesus' followers are no more threat here than in Rome where they slaughtered my brothers. The Romans are here, now, because they want to recapture the Holy City. They were humiliated. Defeated. And that cannot stand."

"Then perhaps you have not heard all you needed to hear from Rome," Anna said.

I pulled on my outer garments. I fought to bend over to slide on my sandals.

"The Emperor blamed you, John. You and your people. They blamed the fire on all of you. And for most of these Romans, they couldn't care less who they murder. To them, you are us. And we are you. You follow Jesus, and Jesus was crucified here. To them, all they remember is the sign Pilate hung above his head. They only know that Jesus was supposed to be the king of us, the King of the Jews."

John sighed. "Perhaps, Anna. Perhaps."

I slowly opened the door, blinking against the bright candlelight. John's shoulders were slumped forward, his hand covering his eyes.

"Perhaps I can speak to the Romans, somehow," John sighed. "Make it clear to them that we follow Christ and have nothing to do with the people here. We are no threat."

Anna stepped forward and cupped John's cheeks in her hands.

"John, no," she said. "That will not help. Are they here to destroy us for taking back our Temple? Perhaps you are right and there is no hope. But there is another factor. Maybe it is different in Ephesus, but among the Romans garrisoned here, those who don't blame us Jews for setting fire to Rome probably already know we and the Christ followers are different. They know this because many of them also follow your Jesus. And they have no allegiance to our people as you once had. They were never Jews as you once were. To the Romans here who believe as you do, we Jews are the ones who made them crucify the Galilean. If Rome is to avenge their city, many of the Romans here in Jerusalem will take vengeance for what happened on that cross. You trying to speak to them is just as likely to make things worse than better, even if they would meet you. You would remind them of what we Jews did to Jesus."

I moved further into the kitchen. Anna and John turned to me. Anna pulled her hands away from his face and backed away from our guest. I looked at John solidly.

"Is that true?" I asked.

I had never thought the pagans of Rome would become Christ followers. And if they had, and they were now threatening the Temple and our people, were not then the Christians also our enemies? I felt the blood warming my face.

John looked at me, then to Anna. He turned back to me and shook his head.

"You were at our gathering. There were some Romans there, the good news is for everyone. But I have no experience in Ephesus with evil thoughts like this. We get along with our Jewish neighbors and they with us. Anyone who truly follows the Lord forgives. It was not a Jewish cross standing above me that day, Rabbi, but a Roman one. Perhaps Romans who have come to faith cannot bear the thought that their own kind put Christ to death. Maybe I should try to speak with them?" He shook his head vigorously. "Perhaps if they hear the call for forgiveness from me, they might in turn protect your people. We follow the same God."

I lifted my right hand. My fingers held my Rabbinic cloak and head wrap. I began to put it on. I looked at Anna for help, but she folded her arms and shook her head.

"John, you have much to do," I said. "You cannot risk yourself. And chances are, you have been away from Israel for so long no one will believe you anyway. I don't care what those Sanhedrin pups said to me earlier, I am going to find a Roman leader out there I can reason with."

"No!" Anna cried. She only then seemed to realize I was not only dressed but heavy laden under my Pharisaical robes.

"Rabbi Nicodemus," John said. "You asked when I first came here if I was scared. You asked because I told you I heard Peter had been killed and then Paul. I am the last. But, what else did I tell you then?"

"That you were not afraid to die," I said.

"Exactly. Do you know why I came to you now? Why it's so important now?"

I shook my head. Anna stared at John, her hands twisting before her.

"I didn't come because I am afraid that I will follow the fate of my friends. I came because I am worried you don't have much time left. None of you have much time. The Romans have made no attempt to hide their intentions. They came here to take back what they believe belongs to the Empire. In Ephesus, we dock their ships all the time. They are making a point to everyone in the Mediterranean, 'Look how we are going to deal with the Jews and their God."

I looked at Anna. Then back at John.

"I must go to the Romans.," I said dryly. "I cannot lift a sword, but I have to do something to protect my people."

Anna snorted a sneering laugh the likes of which I have never heard from my daughter's lips.

"What are you saying?" she shrieked. "No one thinks you can stop the Roman dogs. You weren't even worth the time for the High Priest to see you himself."

"Anna," I said, "he has...."

"Father! Father. The others only made sport of you. Don't you understand? They still hold the grudges of their fathers against you. If they send you to the Romans, it will be as a court clown. They couldn't care less if the Romans sent you back to them in pieces."

I could not look at my daughter. My cheeks burned.

"How dare you," I said. "I am a member of the Sanhedrin. The teacher of the Law. I will speak to whoever I want, and they will listen to me!"

I straightened, though I still stood a bit shorter than Anna. She ran both her hands into the hair above her ears. She was crying now, shaking.

John then said, "Rabbi, I know you are a leader of the people and you love the Temple. The Passover is upon us and you have much on your mind. But I have to beg you...."

"What?" I demanded. My voice was dry. With every sob I heard from Anna, my anger grew. How dare she tell me, in front of John no less, that the others mocked me.

"The Romans are here." John said. "You know this. There are two legions out there now, and my people say another troop marches here from the west. The emperor's own son leads the army. They come here with one purpose. To destroy everything."

My home fell silent for a moment. Then, as if on cue, we heard Roman commands echo through the streets. Horns blew in the distance.

"Then what do you suggest?" I asked.

"We have to leave."

"Leave?" Anna cried. "Leave where? We no longer have anywhere to go. The vineyard was sold long ago. Our only hope is to go into the Temple. Behind the walls and away from these Romans."

"No!" John said. "Jesus told us this day would come. He said we are not to seek false safety behind human walls but have faith in God alone and flee to the hills. That is our path."

"Never," I said. "God will protect all who flee under the shelter of his strong arm. I will not betray my people again!"

"Betray? Rabbi, this decision is not about you. Or me. What about Anna? What about Miriam?"

"Miriam," Anna repeated. She turned around in a full circle, dropping her cup. Cool water splashed across the floor and stuck my feet.

"Miriam!" she shouted. "Oh, no! Where is she? Where is my daughter?"

It was not unusual for her to miss our evening meals, I thought. Especially when her duties caring for the animals in the Temple took up more and more of her time at Passover.

"She is with her friends working in the Temple."

"Then I will find her," John said. "Please, you must pack only what you absolutely need, and be ready to leave immediately when I return."

"You will be caught if you go alone," I said. "I will go. I know the Temple best."

Anna stomped to my side. My walking stick leaned up against the edge of the table. She took it and threw it across the room.

"I have fought to keep you alive, father. You will not go out there, not with the Romans gathering. You will find no friend among them nor among our leaders."

"Anna...."

"Father! You will not leave this house. You try for the Roman camp and it is a suicide march. You go to the Temple now, and you're more than likely to be trampled to death by all the people and livestock going in for the Passover."

She squeezed my hands in her own. I noticed only then how my hands shook. She leaned her forehead against mine.

"You have done so much for our people," she whispered, "and for Miriam and me. Even if you have never been given credit for your efforts, I know. We both know. You have no responsibility to go on a hopeless path. I need you. Here, safe with me."

I let her lift the me-'il off my shoulders. I sat quietly on a cushion and covered my face with my hand.

Just then, Miriam rushed through our front door. She told us she and her friends walked across the Temple to look over the Upper City. Just as John said, a third and much larger Roman army had appeared.

John went room by room, closing our shutters and doors. He went to the courtyard, looking over the rear stone fences into our neighbors' yards.

"I urge you all to stay here the rest of the day. I have to go into the city and prepare my own people to leave. I know you want to go out there and do something. I know Passover is also upon us and you have many responsibilities. But all that has to be put aside."

He left then, shutting the door firmly behind him. The three of us sat in silence as the afternoon passed into a dim but loud evening. Torches lit the entire top of the Temple walls as our leaders moved along with the celebrants here for Passover as if they could protect themselves from the Romans by simply ignoring them. The Romans, for their part, waited in near silence.

Chapter 19

Anna

Passover.

The word is mystical among our people. Pointing both to freedom and our long struggle ahead. Never was the symbolism as real as it was this day.

Not long after the sun rose, we heard a massive roar outside our home, then the pounding of hundreds of feet in the lane beyond our door.

A few minutes later we were started by a sudden and heavy knock. Anna rushed to the door and opened it only a crack. I heard Abram's deep voice. Anna opened the door and Miriam's betrothed rushed in, shutting the door behind him and leaning against it. He gathered himself, came to my side and knelt.

"You must stay here," he said. "With Anna and Miriam. I have been called to the Temple. We were all told to bring our weapons."

He stood and rushed back to the door. His scabbard hung oddly off his belt. He pulled on his helmet, a size too small and riding high on his head.

"Miriam is not with us," Anna said. "I tried to warn her. I didn't want her to leave the house today, but it is Passover. She went to her friends even before dawn."

Abram stopped and leaned his forehead against the door. "To the Temple? She can't... Mother Anna, I will find her right away and send her back. I swear!"

He spun, metal and leather cracking and clanging. He rushed out the door, leaving us in sullen silence. I felt an urge to follow my soon-to-be grand son-in-law, but my body reeled. I sat, and Anna sat heavily next to me, covering her eyes and forehead behind her wrinkled hands.

Eventually, the noon hour arrived. I placed a few bites of bread in my mouth, only because I felt sure this was about to be a very long day.

John arrived early in the afternoon and brought us the first terrible news. Those in the Upper City watched a third Roman legion approach from the west, trampling the area surrounding Golgotha, even knocking down the dozen unused crosses. The hammering of siege towers being built rolled over Jerusalem.

"John," I said. "Please help me to the roof."

I had not been on my roof for years, but Anna kept it tidy. The light was blinding, and the sun warmed my arms. The stairwell to the roof opened toward the west. Since my home was close to the Temple wall, we were higher than most. Maybe two dozen rows of rooftops descended into the valley below toward the south and east before the land rose again into the Mount of Olives.

As I turned around toward the north, the horizon was dark under the smoke of many fires. Below the smoke we could see hundreds of banners blowing in the faint breeze. All about stood thousands of soldiers, some fully ready for battle, others lining up in various formations for the march.

John and I looked down into the lanes and alleys below. My fellow Jews, by threes and fours, rushed toward the road that ringed the outer wall of the Temple. The cobbled stones covered a width of maybe thirty feet out from the base of the structure. As the larger groups of men made it to the road, a cry of encouragement rose from the guards looking down from the top of the wall. Some of the men on the road waved knifes over their heads, some held clubs, a few brandished dull, broad-edged swords. They milled about, shouting approval to each other and then, as if hearing some silent command, they all turned and ran south as the road dipped along the Temple wall.

"Why are they going that way and not into the Temple through the East Gate?" I asked.

"Look," John said. He pointed back to where the East Road entered the Temple through the gate.

The gate was wide open to receive the Passover pilgrims and sacrificial animals. In the mouth, dozens of Temple guards motioned frantically with their arms. We watched them scream their commands but heard nothing above the din created by tens of thousands of people and creatures moving upon the road. Roman horns began to echo off the walls from the north.

We heard Anna's voice crying, "Father!"

John and I looked at each other, then down the stairwell into my home. No one was there.

"Father!" Anna called again. This time it sounded as if it was from the lane at the front of our home.

I turned and moved to the edge of the roof carefully, holding my hand out for John to steady. Down below was Anna, looking up at me with alarm.

A sudden and sure dread boiled within me. Before I could speak, Anna called up again.

"John, stay with father! I am going to bring Miriam home. Abram obviously can't find her. I'll retrieve them both and bring my daughter home!"

"Anna, no!" I shouted. But my daughter had already turned and moved swiftly down the lane.

John stepped back toward the stairwell as if to go after her. He then came back to the edge of the roof and paced back and forth.

Within ten minutes, we saw Anna reach the road to the west of us, near the bottom of the Temple wall. Her gray veil blew back in the gathering wind. She walked with the slight limp in her left hip, holding her arms out as if to balance herself. Instead of turning toward the southern end of the Temple like the men had, she turned uphill, toward the north. Toward the East Road, the Temple gate and, beyond that, the Roman camp. The gate was her quickest route to Miriam.

John and I watched for a quarter of an hour until we could no longer see her among a swarm of people circled around the gate. I couldn't stand the sun for long, so I retreated down the steps and sat upon the highest stair within the shade.

Sometime later, John suddenly called out. I rose with a grunt and went again to the edge of the roof. There! Stumbling among the rocks on the side of the road were two figures. As they came closer, my old eyes recognized the clothing of both Anna and Miriam. They had lost their head scarfs. Anna's graying hair seemed almost white in the reflection of the sun. Miriam's long, dark hair blew across her face from the winds coming now more steadily from the north.

Within minutes I heard their voices on the street. Arguing. Anna's stern voice. Miriam nearly hysterical.

John helped me down the stairs. We opened the front door just as my two girls approached from the left. Miriam came directly to me, squeezing me painfully in a tight hug. She cried. I couldn't understand her words. Anna stood next to John, holding both of his hands between them, deep in discussion.

"What is it?" I asked.

Anna looked at me. She released John's hands.

"I have to go," John said. He wrapped a small cloth around his head, pulling a strip before his face. "Anna said they are closing off the Lower City. My people will be trapped. I have to help them."

He stepped toward the door and grabbed his large walking stick. He paused and turned his head to look at me. "You must all pack, now! And pack light. We must leave the city by nightfall."

With that, John walked into the blinding white street.

"No, no, no!" Miriam yelled. She pushed herself free of my arms and I gasped a breath. "I will not leave! I told you! I will not leave Abram! I will not lose another husband!"

I placed my hand gently upon her shoulder. I looked at Anna and she at me.

"I've been telling her since we left the Temple," Anna said. "I don't know where Abram is, he might be on the other side of the Temple for all we know. Everyone was screaming 'there's another legion coming toward town'. Flaming arrows flew into the Upper City. They called all the men to the Temple."

"Miriam," I said, as quietly as my racing heart would allow. "Your mother is right. Abram would want you to wait here. We must leave while there is time. He will find his way to us."

Miriam stepped back and stared at me. "What are you saying? Abram will be killed! What chance do they have against the Romans?"

"Daughter," Anna said.

"Miriam," I interrupted. "Do not forget yourself. Can our guards beat the Romans? Of course not. But they are in the Temple, and there is no Temple in the world with walls so thick and strong. Do you dare question the Lord? He is our strength. This is his Temple. He will not fail us."

Miriam sighed heavily and dropped to the floor. She sat, sobbing, her face up toward the ceiling.

"I will not leave without him," she said. "I will not lose another husband."

Anna grabbed my hand. She waited for me to speak.

"Miriam," I said. "You have to..."

Miriam looked at me like a wild dog. She was struggling to breathe.

"I will not leave without him," she said with sudden coldness. "You rely on the Lord to protect the Temple? Then I will stay here and wait for Abram and I will trust the Lord will also protect me."

Anna stared at Miriam. A tear trickled down the side of her face and fell from her chin. Her lower lip trembled. She knelt unsteadily before my granddaughter.

"Miriam, I don't understand much about what John has told us. But he is right. When the Romans first came here, I was sure they just wanted to scare us. But if it is true there are now three legions here....don't you understand? They mean to kill us all."

"That's what I mean, mother!" Miriam said. "If they intend to kill us all, they will start with Abram and the other guards. I cannot live if he dies. I cannot!"

Anna sighed. She stood and stepped toward Miriam.

"I cannot!" Miriam shouted again. She looked at me, dark eyes ringed by tears and pleading. But what could I do?

"Your grandfather is too old," Anna said to her daughter. "He will die out there. And you are not leaving this house. Abram is a soldier; he will fight, and God will protect him."

My heart thudded in my chest, hearing my daughter defend the sovereignty of our God.

"Did he protect our husbands?" Miriam protested. "Did he?"

I was caught shocked, to hear her speak this way. But, it was

153

true, wasn't it? What promise could I give her that I didn't give to her and Anna several years ago the night both their husbands fell? They too were good men. Israelites, fighting to protect the Temple and our people.

Dead.

"If he dies," Miriam growled, "then so will I."

With that she pulled up her dress and stormed to the door. My daughter, moving faster than I could ever remember, crashed by her and thudded into the door. She turned, her arms stretched behind her across the width of the frame.

"You will not leave this home!" she shouted.

"Mother!"

"I have lost everything," Anna said. "I will not lose you. You will stay here and protect your grandfather. I will go to the gate and find Abram. If you found him, he would not come with you, to do so would be to destroy his honor. But I will soon be his mother-in-law, he will listen to me. I promise you, I will bring him back. But you must stay here. Protect your grandfather. Prepare some food and water. Be ready to leave the instant I come back. There is no protection from the Romans here. Do you understand?"

"Yes, mother," Miriam said. She looked at me and then crawled to my side, hugging my leg and resting her cheek upon my knee.

Anna stared at me as she wrapped a new veil around her mouth and nose. All I could see were her beautiful dark brown eyes.

I reached out to her. She looked at my hand, then grasped me in a tight hug. Her body shook within my arms. I fought to breathe and kissed her forehead.

"You...," I whispered, but Anna already broke free and turned for the door. She rushed out beneath darkening skies and disappeared down the lane.

Miriam and I went again to the rooftop. Northward was utter chaos. A mass of people pooled before the East Gate. Thousands of arms waved plaintively to the guards on top of the wall. Making things much worse, hundreds of bulls, rams, and lambs clogged the road. About half a mile east of the gate, the river of pilgrims approaching the Temple seemed to part as if around a massive rock. Those to the left of the parting continued with renewed panic toward the Temple, while those to the east of the split flowed suddenly south off the road, tumbling down the embankment and being forced directly toward our homes.

It was then that I first saw Anna. She had not gone toward the Temple road, which was full of armed men rushing back and forth. Instead, she walked due north through the village and upon the East Road. Now, she was holding her veil upon her head against the smoke-filled wind and stumbling close to the Temple gate. Miriam screamed to her. I squeezed her hand for nothing we could say now could ever reach her mother's ears over the distance and the din.

Suddenly, I felt as if someone was in our home. I turned just in time to see John's head rise above the level of our roof as he ran up the stairs.

"I can't find any more of my people," he shouted. "I think they already moved south. Rabbi, we must leave. Now! The Romans are approaching the Upper City. They are moving their towers and catapults."

Catapults, I thought. The Romans had indeed come to break down the Temple walls and destroy us all.

"We can't go yet," I whispered.

"What?" John yelled, rushing to our sides. "Why?"

"We can't go!" Miriam shouted. She pointed toward the road. "My mother is there. She's going to find Abram. We can't leave without them."

John rushed to the side of the roof, leaned against the tiled edge and stared toward the East Road, the Temple, the Romans in the distance. He turned back to us, his eyes wide.

"Miriam," he said. "She'll never find Abram. If it is God's will that he survives, he will have to come and find you. But we cannot stay."

"I will not leave him!" Miriam screamed.

John grabbed her upper arms and glared at her, his face just inches away. "We have to go! We have to get your mother and flee this place. If we don't go now, not only will Abram be lost, but we will lose your mother as well."

John looked back at me. I raised my trembling finger toward the gate. Try as I might, I could not find Anna again within the mass of people and animals pressing harder and harder against the Temple. To my right, thousands of people and beasts overflowed the sides of the road. A dozen rows of Rome's troops breached the road, turning both east and west, directly into the faces of the pilgrims.

A lit arrow arced over the East Road, flying roughly in our direction from the north. Within moments, horns blew loudly from the Roman camp. As if in haunting echo, other horn blasts came over the Temple from the direction of the Upper City.

At the gate, the Temple guards established a half-circle extending twenty or thirty feet out from the wall. But this human wall suddenly collapsed before the weight of those pushing against it. Additional guards appeared at the top of the wall. Within moments, archers shot down into the crowd of pilgrims! Shooting our own people. Shooting into the crowd into which Anna disappeared!

I soon realized the archers were trying only to take down the livestock. As rams and goats and oxen fell, guards formed a new line across the width of the gate, metal shields linked before them. They pushed their way out from the gate, creating just a bit of open space so others could push and pull the animals off the road. A few dozen people climbed over the carcasses and rushed through the gate. I could not find Anna among them.

The panic grew beyond the strength of the guards. The Romans marching toward the gate from only a half mile away slammed their swords against their shields. Horsemen raised up their steeds, heeled them forward, swooping back and forth on the edges of the road. They did not dare come yet within range of the archers, but they didn't need to.

Arrows zipped into the area in front of the gate. This time, the temple guards were not targeting animals, they were forcing back our people so the guards outside the Temple could make it back within.

A massive roar rolled over us from directly to the north. The Romans forced thousands of pilgrims off the road and directly toward our homes. Carts toppled left and right, throwing children and the elderly to the ground. Hundreds of animals ran this way and that, stampeding those in their way.

The door crashed open below us. Miriam turned in front of me, blocking my body from the stairwell with her own. John stepped toward the stairwell, fists clenched. We heard the clank of armor, the stamping of booted feet coming up to the roof.

Miriam cried out, "Abram!"

She pushed me to the side, just hard enough to force me to reach for the tiled roof to steady myself. Miriam turned back to me with alarm. I held my other hand up to her, telling her I was fine, and she turned back toward the stairs. Abram rushed to her and swallowed my granddaughter in an embrace. Miriam covered his face with kisses.

"I am so glad you are here," Abram said.

"I wasn't going to leave without you!"

"You should have, you should have! I ran through all the alleys south of here, telling everyone to leave. The Romans are about to march. We have to get to the southern gates; they might still be open."

I stepped toward the two young ones.

"Abram."

"Yes, father," he said, releasing Miriam and bowing his head.

"We were not going to the Temple," I said. "John insists we leave to the east or south. He thinks the Romans are planning to destroy the city."

"Yes," Abram said. He stopped short, his eyes rising above my shoulder. He pulled Miriam tight.

I spun around, carefully balancing myself. A stream of bodies now moved through the dusty lanes below us. But behind them, thousands of pilgrims scattered before a wave of scarlet cloaked Roman soldiers. The Roman shield walls raised up, pointed spear heads shoving back and forth in the air before them. Step by step, they climbed over bodies on the road and came ever closer to the Temple gate. Directly toward Anna.

"Contend, O Lord," I said the words of the psalm, "with those who contend with me; Fight against those who fight against me. Take hold of buckler and shield and rise up for my help."

Horses, five across, rode into the crowd from north of the gate. Another charge broke over the East Road directly north of us, then swung along the southern edge of the roadway. Angry horns blew again and again.

"Contend, O Lord," I growled.

Miriam and Abram approached me, both reciting the psalm with me time and again. John stepped beside me, his head hung low, his lips moving in silent prayer.

Bodies piled up outside the East Gate, some moving, most still, trampled in the panic of both person and animal. Arrows flew into the people from the direction of the Roman camp. Deeper and deeper, more of the people fell into a silent pile before the gate.

Another group of my neighbors gathered maybe a quarter mile south of the gate along the base of the wall. Several hundred, some armed, many only with sticks. With an unsure cry, they rushed northward up the road, climbing toward the Romans. Soon, they collided with the panicked souls rushing south away from the gate. The armed men turned off the road and headed across the barren recesses in the ground directly toward the first ranks of Romans, pressing ever closer to the gate.

The ground shook under the stamp of the war-horses riding full speed toward the mass of women and children still trapped outside the Gate. Large rocks spun over and over out of the darkened northern sky, bouncing off the wall above and around the Gate. They ricocheted, crashing upon whoever still moved below. Several large stones tumbled south along the road, slicing through the armed men vainly rushing north. Roman cavalry swords moved up and down into the remaining crowd with horrible precision.

"Mother!" Miriam screamed.

"Where?" Abram asked.

She pointed toward the pile of bodies strewn around the base of the Gate. The horsemen soon ran out of prey and wheeled around the outer edge of the carnage. They shouted and charged again, this time into the hundreds, if not thousands, of Jewish men running northward to their deaths in defense of their people and their Temple. As a parent hearing their child's cry amid a dozen others, for a moment I thought I heard, clearly heard, my baby scream for me, though there was nothing but a rising, rolling blast of agony from the Gate.

I shouted the psalm over and over, holding my arms out wide. My voice cracked until it gave out. My trembling arms fell to my sides. I crumbled to the stony roof. Stinging tears dripped into the dust.

Where are you, Lord? I thought.

"I have to go," Abram said. For a moment, my heart leapt.

Yes! I thought desperately.

I looked at the young man. Miriam gripped his cloak tightly with one hand, hitting his shoulder with the butt of her other fist.

"No, no, no...," she sobbed.

I pushed myself up and stumbled toward them, grimacing against the horrors I heard behind me.

Looking at Abram, I paused. The image of Anna's dark eyes floated before me.

"No!" I said. "She went to find you, for Miriam's sake. You will not sacrifice yourself. It....it is....too late. Both of you, go downstairs, grab what water and food you can. We must leave. Now."

"I would not be able to live with myself," Abram said firmly. He received another of Miriam's blows in his open hand and gently moved her arm down to her side. He began to pull away from her.

"Stop!" I screamed with all my remaining breath.

Abram looked at me, wide eyed. John raised his head from prayer and stepped closer. Miriam stared at me with confused hope. I felt the looming walls of the Temple behind me, the eyes of God looking down upon this roof. The complete absence of my daughter.

"We are leaving now!" I gasped. "The Romans will come this way next. God forgive me, but we must leave now!"

With that, Abram's resolve melted. He pulled Miriam tight, kissed her roughly on the forehead. He led her in front of me, past John, and down the stairs. I followed behind as quickly as I could, needing both feet to steady me on each step. My legs seemed to be of another body altogether. John reached down the stairs from the roof, helping me as far as he could. He then stood and looked back once more toward the Temple Gate and the East Road.

He turned back to the stairs and, not looking at me, said, "I am so sorry."

Chapter 20

Romans

My heart nearly burst. We stumbled down from the roof and found that Anna had earlier laid out many of my belongings. Abram came to my room and stuffed these into a small satchel.

John slid our heavy table against the front door. Beyond it, we heard screams, hundreds of stumbling feet, a few plaintive knocks. Some of those who passed cried out the names of missing family and friends. Many names of long-time neighbors. Constantly in the background, the drums. Horses. The crash of rock and stone. Metal upon metal. Shouts in that bestial Latin.

We went through our courtyard, past the burnt-out fire pit and to the back wall. Abram lifted himself up and sat atop the head-high stone barrier.

"No one is back here."

He swung his legs over the top of the wall and landed on the opposite side with a grunt. We saw his head and arms pop back over the top of the wall. John lifted our belongings, two bags of clothing, three with food, and a few large skins of water.

John then lifted Miriam. She grabbed Abram's arms and he pulled her over the top of the wall. Just as she fell out of sight, I heard a heavy knock on our front door. I spun, imagining my daughter in the lane, alone, knocking.

John turned to lift me.

"No," I said, looking through the dim shadows of our home. "I will wait for Anna."

John shook his head. The roar of chaos rose from the lane before our home. He pointed in that direction without a word. There was another loud thump on the door and this time the call of a Roman soldier.

"She is not there," John whispered.

I looked back at the stone wall.

"I don't know if I can make it."

John opened his mouth to protest. Then stopped. He looked at me sadly and pointed to my head dress.

"That is a rabbi's turban," he said.

"Yes," I said, reaching up to touch it.

"And your blue cloak. Rabbi, the last thing we want is for you to bring attention to yourself as a leader of the Temple. You cannot wear those."

The world turned quiet and still. I stared at John and shook my head.

"I cannot turn my back on the Lord."

"You are not," John said. "I serve the Lord, Abram serves the Lord. Miriam serves the Lord. The Lord is not served by what you wear."

"But I can't turn my back...."

John stopped me with a withering look. He pointed toward the top of the Temple wall, looming over my home.

"There will be nothing left," he said. "My Lord told us this would be torn down. Don't you understand, you cannot sacrifice yourself over mere pride. If you do not leave, Miriam will not leave. And she will die. And if you wear those clothes, the Romans will kill you. They do not care how old you are. And then they will kill us."

I closed my eyes in prayer, but I could not remember a single psalm. My thoughts were blank except for the recurring image of Anna rushing through the door and into the courtyard.

I slowly lifted my head dress off and placed it upon the cushions near the fire pit. The sweat in my hair instantly chilled me even in the late afternoon air. I pulled off my cloak and placed it next to the turban. The blue cloth and sewn-in scriptures look angrily back at me. I knew I would never again wear that which had distinguished me from all others for nearly seventy years.

The four of us were soon over the wall, out of our neighbor's abandoned home and moving southward as quickly as we could manage. Behind us there seemed to be a lull, either because everyone was dead or because the Romans had had their fill of carnage for the day. All around us, thousands of my neighbors and bewildered pilgrims flowed toward the southern lip of the Mount of Olives. Quiet exhaustion silenced the people of the living God during what was to be our greatest celebration.

The sunset brought a few moments of hope as rows of Temple guards waved torches upon the ramparts of the wall. Word spread from the south that the Huldah and western gates were open. The crowds around us swelled forward, crossing our path and heading toward the southwest. I looked toward the towering walls, which grew in height as the land slopped ever lower. Looking further back, there was a large and growing gap on the road littered only with the shapes and shadows of lifeless bodies. I looked still further north, to the East Gate. The Romans were gone. In their wake, a massive pile of bodies spread a hundred feet in a writhing semicircle.

"Keep going south," John said. "Toward that rise. Don't drift toward the Temple."

"I don't know," Abram said, looking toward the Temple. "If the gates really are open, shouldn't we....?"

"No," John said. His voice betrayed his frustration. For a moment, I almost panicked, sure this follower of Christ would just give up and leave us to our own fates. "We were told to flee the city, to flee to the hills! We cannot go back."

Abram straightened and stood nose to nose with John.

"I am a guard of the Temple."

John grabbed Abram by the shoulder and snapped him back and forth. He spun Abram toward Miriam.

"She," he said very slowly, "will die. Nicodemus will die. You will die. This is not a discussion. We will hide in the hills and we will not go back toward the Temple."

With that, he let Abram go, slung all the water skins over his shoulder and gripped the satchel with our food under his arm. He strode steadily southward in the darkening fields. Abram stood still for a moment, then reached a hand out to Miriam and the two of them followed John.

Evening fell early under the dark clouds of smoke. Our progress toward the rising slopes of the mount slowed. We paused only once to test a battered cart left beside our path in a rock filled gully. Abram and John tried to pry the wheels lose but in doing so the wheel on the right fell off and plunked into a small stream. Miriam sat next to me, taking small sips from our water skin. I wrapped my arm around her and felt her shiver. I fought through my foggy thoughts and recited the psalm seeking the Lord's help:

> I say to the LORD, "You are my God."
> Hear my cry for help, Lord!
> My Sovereign Lord, my strong
> defender, you have protected me in battle.
> LORD, don't give the wicked what they
> want; don't let their plots succeed.

Abram rejoined us as John went off to scout the path ahead. His face looked decades older in the gloom. He stared over our shoulders toward the Temple. Suddenly, a burst of orange reflected off his sweaty brow.

A boom echoed over the valley from the north. Another, deeper thump answered from farther off. The first sound replied, then the second. Back and forth. I struggled to my feet and turned toward the Temple. The south end was only a half-mile or so away from us. The Huldah Gates looked like dark mouths swallowing the thousands who had gathered before them searching for safety.

"Oh, good Lord," Miriam gasped. She let go of my upper arm and leaned into Abram's embrace. He met her with strong arms. His hand cupped the back of her head.

A series of flaming arrows streaked up from the East Road. Moments later, another set arced over the Temple from the Roman camp. Within minutes, fires sprang from the rooftops in our village, slowly marching south toward our home. In the firelight, company after company of Romans stacked up. What we thought might be the end of hostilities for the day was simply a pause. To clear the bodies in front of the East Gate perhaps. To clear the way for the Roman battering rams.

The booming continued. Massive clouds of dark smoke lifted high into the sky. The tops of these bitter clouds turned to blood as the sun dipped over the western horizon.

"Come!" John shouted. "It is getting too dark to see our path. We must hurry or we'll be trapped in these fields!"

Halfway up the mount, screams rose behind us. Like Lot to his wife, we warned each other not to pause, nor to turn to look. For a few moments, we were trapped behind a small rock wall, inaccessible behind a five-foot-wide stream. Abram dragged several downed saplings from the field beside us and built a small walkway over the water. John helped the three of us over the stream and wall. He paused and looked back. I watched his dark shadow frozen before a scene my mind could not comprehend. He turned back and pulled me up the slope.

The olive plants were not yet fully in bloom so the path before us was relatively clear. We found a recently plowed furrow, which provided a straight and easy walk up the side of the hill. As we climbed, I heard invisible shadows surrounding us, moaning or sobbing in the night. Here and there, we heard the cry of someone in pain, the inconsolable shriek of a young child. The wind blew toward us from the north, carrying with it the sounds of the terrible battle, the warmth of still growing fires, and the awful, indescribable stench of burning flesh.

Just when I thought I could not take another step, John turned and brought us to a stop. Abram tossed down the two large sacks he carried. Miriam dropped to the ground, pulling her knees up before her. She covered her head with her hands. I took a step toward her, but Abram sat by her side and wrapped his arm around her shoulders.

John stood off a few feet to my side, looking into the night sky. The clouds of smoke almost entirely blotted out the stars.

"What are we to do?" I asked.

John looked toward the Temple. Far off, the East Gate was ablaze. The Gate and its arch were gilded in silver and yet a ring of flames poured out from the opening.

John pointed at it. "I think they used the ram to batter off the

165

metal. Look, the wooden gate within has caught fire."

I squeezed my hands into fists. In the light of the flames engulfing the Gate, row after row of Roman troops crouched behind their shield walls. Large catapults launched flaming bags or large stones upon and over the wall. Hundreds of smaller arrows and darts danced through the air toward the ramparts, driving back the last of the Temple guards who had responded with their own arrows and stone.

We saw the ram swing back once more, then heard a cracking boom. A great blast of sparks tumbled from the now shattered Gate over the first rows of Romans. A cheer taunted us, and rank after rank of Romans rushed through the now open Gate. They paused for maybe ten minutes, their initial troops certainly facing the guards within. Soon, the entire Roman legion moved smoothly into the bowels of the Temple.

The Romans did not seem interested in risking their cavalry within the confines of the Temple. Instead, a great host, maybe hundreds strong, galloped toward us down the road at the base of the wall. The high-pitched cries of several women carried across the field.

"Anna," I sighed.

John reached for my arm. I knew what he was going to say, but I could not bear to hear it or see what might be in his eyes.

Instead, a horrific cry rose from the Temple. Those gathered at the southern gates realized their peril from the Roman cavalry. At the same moment, I huge plume of fire and sparking ash rose behind the top of the Royal Portico built high above the southern end of the Temple. The portico's flat roof interrupted the path around the top of the wall above the Huldar gates, rising ten feet or more above a wide series of columns.

"What could burn so brightly within the Temple?" John asked.

"The hay," Abram said. "There are thousands of bundles down below for feeding the Passover animals."

As the immediate glow of the fire dimmed, we saw hundreds of figures standing upon the roof of the portico. Women, veils blowing back from the wind of the fires set below them upon the Temple courts. Many seemed to have their arms crossed in front of them, holding the small dark shapes of their babies and children.

The Roman horsemen were busy at work at the base of the wall, cutting their way through the people and remaining guards in front of the southern gates. Then, marching in file around the southern tip of the Temple from the Upper City to the west, another legion of soldiers descended upon my hapless countrymen. They had not even bothered to unscabbard their swords. Their archers, marching haphazardly through the rough edge of the road, loosed arrow after arrow into the crowds. Within moments, the two Romans armies met and raised a rough cheer against the Temple wall. They brought fuel and fire to the southern gates and lit them ablaze. The tens of thousands of Jews who had been forced from this path of hoped-for safety stampeded down the southern road, the very road upon which I had led Herod's troops toward Bethlehem so long ago.

The growing fires licked up beyond the Royal Portico. People by the thousands crowded upon that flat rooftop. Their final refuge was now a trap. Flames and smoke hemmed them in until they formed a dark wall of moving specters, arms raised here and there, dancing before the fire.

Then, the first body fell from the portico. The person's long dark shadow traced a spinning path down the Temple Wall before hitting the ground below. The person dropped some sixty feet to the base of the gates and crashed upon some of the Romans.

Another fell, then another. One body tumbled down from the edge of the portico, robes ablaze.

We watched the Roman troops back away from the gates. Their horses rode wildly left and right. Body after body now crashed down. A few women fell, losing grip of their children on the way to the pavement below.

Then we heard the jeering. The horrible chant echoing off the walls of the Temple. The Romans called up.

"Salito! Salito!"

"Jump," I muttered.

Jump.

Chapter 21

Vineyard

"Father, grant me the wisdom of the Spirit."

John's deep voice was so tired and gravely I could barely make out his words. He marched on through the dark, always in the lead, kicking stones and mumbling warnings to us. We stumbled around the western edge of a hill.

"John," Abram whispered. "This land is rising. Even in the dark we might be seen moving against the starlight. Stay behind that outcropping of rock to your right."

We no longer saw the fires blazing above and around the Temple. Just the flickering glow against the smoke-filled sky. As we began to swing toward the east and north, thousands of our countrymen fled south from the city along the road toward Bethlehem. Now and then, Romans surrounding the southern gates grew bored at the spectacle and charged a mile or more down that road, scattering the refugees before them.

In the mid of night, we finally rested. Miriam and Abram huddled together under a small tree. I struggled to catch my breath as John walked off into the dark. Later, he returned, telling us of half a dozen abandoned carts strewn along the path. He had dragged one most of the way back to us, but he couldn't make it up the hillside. The three of us stood, the cold evening wind nipped at us beneath our cloaks. We hobbled down to the cart, my old man's feet screaming at me with each step.

Abram and John helped Miriam and me into the back of the cart and each took a handle. The two quietly debated for a few minutes over which way to go. John wanted to go south and then west to reach the shore of the sea where he thought we'd be able to find a boat to return to his land. Many of his people already left the Holy City over the last few days following the same route. He was sure we would find others to help us with the difficult travels ahead.

Abram, however, wanted to go south to the other Jewish towns to find members of the Temple guard who might have survived.

Miriam and I knew the course we should go. I was too tired to argue, but Miriam was firm.

"We will go the east," she said. "Around the back edge of this hill and then head north. We know those lands very well. Our old vineyards are not far. Just past the East Road."

Eventually John agreed with Miriam, telling Abram we could then continue past the vineyards and enter the far north. We'd be able to track by the Jordan River and return to the Galilean lands of his birth. From there, he said, he'd take us to the safety of his adopted hometown, Ephesus.

"I'm not going farther north than our vineyard," I said. "It is not ours anymore, but I know the owners well and I'm sure they will let us wait there. Just in case. Anna..."

Whatever the thoughts of the other three, they were far too tired for further discussion. Perhaps the simple thought of a welcoming home, a bed and food were all we could hope for at that moment. To me, however, as my sight turned to the still raging destruction behind us, we just had to get away from the stench blown into our faces from the heated winds.

There is a small dirt road running around the southern tip of the Mount of Olives. As we rounded and bent back toward the east, the landscape rose to our left, blocking our site of the Temple. We sank into a deep darkness. We could hear others hidden in the dark aimlessly stumble across the lands. Once in a while, someone risked lighting the torch and twice we caught the dark outlines of small homes and barns outlined against the sky. The smoke-filled air let no light through from the moon and stars.

After a couple hours ride, the sky lightened just a bit with the colors of dawn. Instead of bringing comfort, I felt trapped, a prey now caught in the open. The path continued north, and we approached the crossing with the East Road. Abram and John pushed the cart past the road and onto a side path. They hid us under a few low trees, and we rested until the sun fully crested the eastern horizon.

Once the sun rose, John stood and stretched. He walked up to a small knoll and soon returned.

"There are people approaching on the road from Jerusalem."

"Romans?" Abram asked.

"No, I don't think so. But I think it best if we stay out of sight of everyone out there, best we can."

I nodded. "Miriam, we should get out of the cart and lessen the burden on our very tired guides. We only have a few hundred paces to go before that dirt path breaks off to lead us into our old vineyard."

I reached out for my granddaughter's hand, but she would not take it. She slid off the back of the cart and leaned her hands against it to help push. I walked several steps behind her, now utterly alone, wrapping my arms around my midsection for warmth.

Perhaps an hour later we turned right and walked down a long weed-infested lane. We passed through a rough wooden fence. To the left and right, long rows of brown, withered vines stretched into the distance. Most of the leaves had been plucked and only a few small buds were visible in the spring air. Before us, a modest home was nestled between two rising hillsides. The home I myself had built. We passed through an outer stone fence and onto a tiled patio. We knocked on an open wooden door. When there was no answer, Abram walked all around the home and returned from the opposite side.

"There's no one here," he said. "Smoke is still rising from the fire pit in the courtyard so whoever was here fled rapidly sometime since last night. I looked in the kitchen, there is some half-eaten food. Maybe the people who lived here went to the Temple for Passover. Maybe they just packed up and fled before the Romans came this way."

We walked into the main house, what used to be my house!, and then into the center courtyard. Everything was as Abram described.

All the livestock was gone. A large cart waited, half laden with supplies, but left behind. Inside, several candles still burned toward the end of their wicks.

John scouted the remaining rooms. He reported there were warm clothes, some sandals and several large skins already filled with water. I could picture the man I sold my home to, Timothy, and his wife. I wondered if they still owned these vineyards. As we had approached, I hoped the house would feel like out home again, but instead all seemed foreign, barren and sad.

We washed the grime off our faces in a trough and then climbed to the rooftop. We stared at the black pillar of smoke rising from the Temple. The opposite of the white pillar of cloud God sent to Moses to lead our people here in the first place. Small groups wandered in our direction. There were two larger gatherings, one straight ahead and one some way off to the south. Each began with maybe thirty or forty people but grew by the minute as we watched. Behind them, the sun reached the top of the Temple wall. The low hanging smoke was so dense, we could see nothing except the specs of a few Roman horsemen moving north and south at the base. The tops of the smoke-filled clouds blazed a dark, angry red in the morning sun.

Thousands of goats and rams and oxen roamed the lands between us and the city. Sacrifices meant for the holy Temple, now shepherdless and strangely silent.

John turned to the three of us.

"We can't stay here long."

"Look around," I said. "The Romans aren't coming this way. They don't care for anything but the Temple and the Holy City. Nothing has been damaged here in this home."

"That's right," Miriam said very quietly.

There was something in her voice that made me turn toward her with concern. Abram reached for her hand and leaned over to whisper into her ear. She snatched her hand away and stepped back from her betrothed. I reached out for her, suddenly afraid she'd back up and fall into the inner court of the home. She looked at me and her eyes were ablaze. She turned herself around in a circle, arms fully outstretched left and right, then stopped, grimacing at me.

"Yes!" she said, "nothing has happened here. No one has died here. Nothing has even been touched!"

She held up her finger and jammed it toward me.

"But my mother is gone. You killed her!" she screamed.

"Miriam," John gasped softly.

"No!" she screamed. "This was ours. This was our home. Our lands. And you sold it. You sold it and you gave the money away, for what? Because the Temple needed something. Some new decoration? Look what good it has done for our people now! They're all gone. The Temple is on fire. She is there, burnt up with the rest of them. She should have been here. Safe! This is all your fault."

Miriam rushed to the stairs and ran down quickly. I heard crashing plates and cups and who knows what else below. Abram followed her. We heard arguing, then whispering, then silence. Then, soft muffled sobs.

I stood like stone. I wanted to go down to talk to my granddaughter, but now she was promised to Abram. And what would I say anyway? I knew she didn't really blame me. But I did. She was correct in every way. My face chilled as the morning breeze passed my now sweaty brow.

I could have kept this farm, couldn't I? I could have kept Anna and Miriam away from the Temple.

John and I stared at the Holy City. I could make out a few points along the East Road as it rose and fell across the countryside. There was a break in the landscape directly ahead, providing a glimpse the East Gate, then the road bent south into a gully cut through the Mount of Olives.

John looked down at me, tears filling his eyes.

"She shouldn't have said that."

"No," I sighed, looking into the sky. "She is right. We would have been safe out here. They came to the city to be with me. I grew old and refused to be away from the Temple. I refused to give up my place among the leaders of our people, even when the Sanhedrin didn't want me. It was my job to protect them, and now Anna is missing."

"I understand," John said. "But you did what you did for God. You can't blame yourself, there's no time for that. We must put aside our anger at each other and leave this place. We must move as quickly as we can northward. Romans might not care about Galilee, and I have people up there, family I still know and people who might help us. But we must go soon. There are already several groups of cavalry moving this way from the Temple. They will come in greater numbers as the morning passes. They won't be satisfied just with the Temple. They aim to wipe out our people."

"Oh, I'm not leaving," I said. "Anna knows if she can't find us at home, we certainly would have come this way. She'll come to our old home. I am not leaving without her."

John clapped his hands very hard in front of him. He looked to the sky and let out a great growl. He turned his sights toward me and walked very close. He looked at each of his hands as he grabbed me purposefully by the shoulders.

"She," he said slowly, "is gone. Rabbi Nicodemus, your daughter is dead. Anna is dead. You know that. You saw her go to the Gate. No one could have survived."

I shook him loose. I stormed to the side of the roof and pointed angrily toward Jerusalem.

"No! She is there! She will come!"

John also pointed toward the west.

"Look!"

Massive flames now licked the sky from within and without the Temple. Black clouds of smoke curled and swelled over the city. A series of horn-calls echoed through the morning air, then suddenly the BOOM, BOOM. Over and over, as if something heavy smashed into solid stone. Which, I understood, was exactly what was happening.

Over the rise which first brought the East Road into our view, I saw a series of tall metal poles. Roman eagles. Roman battle flags fluttering in the wind. Behind them now, many lines of Roman troops, fully armed. A group of them broke off the road to the north, crossing the open land between us and the Holy City. Dozens of our people who had been hiding here and there in the cracks and crevices were forced again to flee. Archers cut some down from behind. Other archers turned to the livestock, bringing them down to later fill their own bellies.

All my prayers had been empty. Unheard. God allowed his

people to be utterly destroyed this day. This Passover. He allowed my Anna to be butchered. I stared at the walls of the Temple that had been the center of my life for over seventy years. Inside, the Holy of Holies. Desecrated. Destroyed.

I stepped back, wishing with sudden clarity that I could be a younger man with the strength to throw myself headlong into those Roman spears. One last empty act to please my Lord.

But as my face burned, I pictured Miriam down below. Sobbing. Deprived of her mother, her home, her people. John looked at me with renewed patience, guessing my thoughts.

"She will not leave without you," he said. "Miriam will die here if you stay. You can still save her. Rabbi, you can save your granddaughter. For her sake and for Anna, you must lead her away from this place. She is angry with you now, but you must lead all of us to the north. There is no time. We must go now.

Chapter 22

The Bitter Ones

For many long weeks, we wound our way past the Sea of Galilee. Marian no longer spoke to me. Abram and John took counsel between themselves and left me little more than a nuisance and silent passenger.

I lost the stability of my spiritual life as one Sabbath after another passed without proper worship. Most of the synagogues up to the Jordan River and into Galilee were closed for fear of the Romans. We found little support in those areas beyond the barest of sustenance. I cannot blame my countrymen because we were far from the only people fleeing the Romans seeking their help. Even though John was now in his fifties, he and Abram helped some of the local fishermen with their work in order to gain the supplies we needed to continue our march northward, out of the promised land and onto foreign soil.

John's goal was Ephesus. As the miles went by, I realized Miriam's only comfort was her time with Abram listening to John's stories about Jesus. I had my own stories, but my mouth was tired and mute. My granddaughter and her betrothed grew more and more excited with the thought that we may be able to join John's people in Ephesus. Abram had done away with his temple uniform and worked by the Sea of Galilee for many days learning from John the tricks of the fisherman's trade.

The problem was getting to Ephesus in both a timely and safe manner. I suggested going to Antioch because this was the traditional place other Jews gathered when they had been driven from the Holy Land. There were rumors of a large synagogue and a vibrant trade in such things as silk. I thought, if anywhere, we would be appreciated for bringing into their community a member of the actual Sanhedrin of Jerusalem.

I was surprised to find John also more than interested in Antioch. He said this was where his friend Peter came on his way to Rome. Saul also stayed in the city up for many years, creating one of the first and more vibrant communities of the Nazarene's church. As we approached Antioch, however, John fell into a brooding silence. Now that we were nearing his adopted people, he fell again under the strain of both his position of leadership and of the task of writing Jesus' story. What would he now write, following God's complete abandonment?

After who knows how many weeks of travel, we finally reached the Orontes River. The summer heat began to fade. On the east side, Antioch bustled with constant activity. We passed Roman baths and public buildings where large mosaics were both ornate and colorful. Almost as colorful were the long locks of silken garments passing back and forth between hundreds of merchants and their customers.

We stopped first at the home of Orrus, a man my friend Joseph had described to me as a trusted colleague. Unfortunately, Orrus had passed away a few years earlier. The hospitality of his children was still apparent, however, and they welcomed us into their spacious home. Orrus' son, Antonio, met us with many warm words, and some coins he gave to help us in our time of need. He spoke to me for hours about our faith and many people from Jerusalem his father had known.

Over dinner that first night, our host told us of the general fear within the Jewish population. There were many rumors that the Roman blood lust had not been fully satisfied in Jerusalem. I was beyond heartbroken as they told me the stories they heard of what happened to the Temple. Some said tens of thousands had been killed, others said as many as half a million lay rotting in the streets of the Holy City. The Temple itself had been burned before the systematic effort of destroying the walls and the courts began in earnest. The concern now in most people's minds was what to do to avoid a similar fate here in Antioch.

We spoke deep into the night, as if all my silence along the long trip to their city had only damned up my words. They explained to John after some initial hesitation that many of the Antiochians blamed him and his fellow Christians for what had happened. The tradesmen of the town who had employees and activities throughout the Mediterranean knew the Romans hated John's people as much they did the Jews.

"It would be very wise," Antonio told John, "for you to avoid the Jewish synagogue altogether. I don't mean to be inhospitable, but there is a large community of your people here, it would be safer for you to find lodging with them."

John agreed and gave our host many thanks. After John retired for the evening, I sensed Antonio turn toward me, the smile leaving his wide face.

"Father Nicodemus," he said, "we're not sure what to do here. We don't know how to explain what's happened. We've long been cut off from our people in Jerusalem, but the Temple? The Temple of the living God? How could this happen? How?"

I looked at the half-empty cup of wine before me for many long minutes. I still had no answer for this one question that had plagued me for since the spring Passover. How could this have happened? This young Antonio looked at me now as a member of the Sanhedrin, an expert in the Law and the scriptures. Expecting me to have his answer. But my certainty had long since died. I was now only disappointed, confused. Angry.

"I am an old man," I told him. "I no longer expect to suddenly find wisdom concerning things God makes so unclear. I've asked myself and God your question hour by hour since Jerusalem fell."

Antonio sat still, expecting much more. I leaned back into my chair and closed my eyes with the impunity of an old man. But inside, my heart raced.

Here I was in a new city, with people who should expect something special from me. But I felt nothing within. The following evening would bring the Sabbath, my first within a real synagogue in many weeks, perhaps months. The thought of that place suddenly filled me both with excitement and dread. With my eyes closed, my body, though refreshed by our meal with Antonio and his family, attacked, bringing thick exhaustion and a dozen points of pain and discomfort.

At the same time, as I opened my eyes and looked up into the shadowed ceiling high above me, I didn't want to sleep. The fresh thoughts about our people's fate brought with them a slowly boiling rage. My hands clenched into fists and I broke into a sweat beneath my embroidered silken robes. I did not want this foreign people in their foreign land. I wanted my people, my land, my Anna! I wanted my revenge.

Was this the rage the people of Bethlehem felt for Herod's men? The way they regarded me when they discovered I was the one who led his soldiers to their bloody task?

The following day passed without incident as our hosts let us sleep. That evening, Sabbath came and with it a tearing headache. I excused myself and, thankfully, fell immediately to sleep. I felt somewhat refreshed with the sunrise and dressed in some of the rabbinic clothing my old friend Joseph had left here of one of his visits, perhaps a decade or more before. The dusty clothes made me sneeze until my ribs ached. Antonio's cart didn't help as it bounced noisily over several cobbled streets toward the synagogue.

Off to the left and right I saw profane temples, evil gathering places. Some Greek, others Roman, others much older still. I could almost smell the stench rising from them. The very air surrounding these vile offenses looked shadowed, even in the bright morning.

We rounded a corner and the cart stopped under a large tree. The wide tops were filled with thick fall leaves, shadowing the street. In the coolness below, we waited and chatted for a few moments. Antonio said that he, as a wealthy businessman within the city, entered the synagogue just before the local Rabbi. Finally, he held out an arm and we walked down a gravel path between well-tended bushes.

I am not sure what I expected, perhaps the type of respect and interest someone of my rank would have demanded. But when we took our seats near the Rabbi, the room was silent, brooding. The Rabbi leaned toward Antonio to inquire as to who I was. He looked at me strangely, sideways with half closed eyes. He nodded, grunted and turned to explain to his people that Antonio had brought a strange and unexpected guest. He asked me to rise, which I did on unsteady legs.

"Here," he said, "is another survivor from the Temple. Why he is here and not in the Holy City is not clear. But our visitor is not only from Jerusalem, he had been a member of the Sanhedrin itself. This is Nicodemus. This is the man we used to hear many stories about."

I half turned toward the two hundred or so men sitting on cushions around the Rabbi and then back to the Rabbi.

"What stories?"

One of the men behind me spoke, "You knew the one called Jesus."

I shook my head. I looked on Antonio. He did not look back at me. I then looked at the Rabbi and raise my hands to my sides in question.

The Rabbi turned to the man who had just spoken to me.

"James," he said, "let us not jump to conclusions. Let our friend speak for himself."

"This Jesus," I said, "I did not even know the man."

There is a general murmuring and the wagging of many heads. A man in the back of the room stood and completely turned his back to me.

"Gentlemen," I said, "I do not know what you have heard. I met this man once; I went out to meet him as an emissary from the Sanhedrin."

"And you also buried him!" another man said. "Joseph told us."

This time when I looked down at Antonio he looked up at me. Our eyes fixed for a moment and he shook his head.

"We heard many stories from Joseph," a third man said. "That traitor who came to our synagogue and then went to the Christians. He was one of them. And you helped bury their false Lord. And now look what has happened."

Antonio stood then. The discussion was taking an unexpected and quick turn and would certainly question his own family's relationship with Joseph.

I held my hand up toward Antonio to still him. He was my host, I had to defend his honor. I took a deep breath and walked next to the Rabbi. I turned to study the faces of those sitting in front of me.

"My brothers, this man, this Jesus. I did speak with him once in private at the behest of our priests. And I later spoke against the sentence of death our high priest pronounced upon him. But I was not his follower. He is not the Messiah."

"Then why did you visit him?" the Rabbi asked. "The Sanhedrin executed him. Blasphemer. Our leaders should have nothing to do with him. You expect us to believe they sent you to speak with the man?"

"My friend," I said. "I was sent because some of us thought this man really was the Messiah. We hoped he would defeat the Romans and raise Israel back to our rightful place."

There were many shouts now and a few curses. Even in the dim room, I could see faces flush with red rage.

"And yet," a man before me said rapidly, "this man did not do away with the Romans. The Romans did away with him! And the memory of him led to the Romans to crush our Holy Temple. What are we to do about all of this, Rabbi?"

I shook my head.

"I do not know."

The man stood and turned to his fellows.

"Stay silent, perhaps?" he asked. "Are we to stay silent as a herd of sheep? Or are we to strike back at the Romans? Strike back at these Christians? My brothers, stand up and serve the living God! Something must be done."

I shook my head again and held my hands up before the men.

"No," I said. "Excuse me but I am an old man. I want revenge upon the Romans as much as any of you. More. Much more. But you cannot fight them."

"Yes, we can!" the man said. "We have the Lord God Almighty on our side."

A few others shouted encouragement. Others looked afraid.

"You cannot...."

"You are no longer a Jew!" the man at the back of the room screamed.

"I lost my daughter to the Romans!" I shouted back. My voice echoed back to me off the walls. I stepped back as if the words punched me in the chest. I realized only then that, even in my rare discussions with Miriam, I had never admitted this horrible fact out loud.

I looked at the men in front of me one by one. My eyes burned with the threat of tears.

"I lost my dear Anna. She sacrificed herself so my granddaughter and I might live. She was caught outside the East Gate, trapped among thousands of others who were trampled and run through like so many wild dogs."

I scanned the men again. Many of the faces who earlier looked timid nodded eagerly as if I alone spoke the obvious truth.

"If you rise up and strike back, you will lose your own daughters. Your own sons. Your own wives. Your own Annas. You will lose this place. You will lose your city and your lives. Our God in heaven did not spare his Holy City. What makes you think he will spare you?"

Antonio stood and walked to my side before anyone else could speak. He pushed me to the door of the synagogue. It grew deathly silent behind. We made it to his cart and rode quickly to his large, cold home. He left again quickly, perhaps to mend some damaged relationships. Within days, he essentially forced me from his home. The ire of his fellow Jews in the city was too much for him to risk. He ever so politely lodged me with a poor Jewish couple close enough to the wharf to fill my days and nights with the smell of fish. The couple's polite interest was more than enough, however, to slowly revive my body, if not my spirit.

Besides, I had Miriam and Abram to worry about and they were more important than the fate of this synagogue which had clearly forgotten our ways. Miriam was seldom with me, refusing now to join even our sparse Sabbat. Mingling more and more freely with John's people.

John found me and even brought a few scrolls from the prophets. Occasionally, when the wind died down, I would open them and read by the seashore. I started in Exodus, wanting perhaps to feel again the great power of our God. But, over and again, I would return in dry sadness to Job or the psalms.

Once or twice, John arrived with small sections of what he was writing about Jesus. He had employed a local scribe to copy Saul's letter which he had read to the gathering in Jerusalem, and the man was helping John now with his task. The man's hand was smooth enough for even my old eyes to read.

I read with some eagerness at first a long section John wrote about his last meal with his Lord. There was so much there, a new covenant, a promise of protection, a call to love. Even to love one's enemies. But as I read on my stomach began to ache, my neck tightened. I knew where this accounting would end. In the courts where I did nothing more than speak up weakly for this man. And upon a stone hill. And within a stone tomb.

Later, John came with the portion of his story which recounted my own meeting with Jesus. John retold his friend's words, that the Spirit would go where it would, like the wind. That God loves the whole world. That the Spirit does not go only to that which comes from the flesh. That God might not only be with me and my people. Did that mean that the Spirit was also with the Romans, with those who slaughtered my Anna?

Weeks passed as I waited, essentially banished from my own people. I feel into a deeper sadness. Even when Miriam and Abram surprised me for dinner, I could not eat, nor bear to listen to them talk. Finally, Abram asked me what we should do. Should we stay in Antioch? Should we try to go back home? Should we move on with John, since he planned to continue to Ephesus now that the spring sailing weather approached.

I couldn't answer. I thought only about the coming Passover, just a few weeks away. That week would always now stand as a yearly reminder of the time Anna died! Would we find ourselves this Passover without a place even to celebrate the moment God freed his people and brought them upon that great and horrible trek?

One evening John stopped by. We retired to a small fire burning at the edge of the sandy seashore. The wood from this area burned sweet and tickled my nose. I watched a few young boys throw rocks at the gulls finding the leftovers of the falling tide. Not much older, I suppose, than those boys murdered by Herod with my help.

"Rabbi Nicodemus," John said. "I need to ask you once more about Jesus. When I return to Ephesus, I will need to read what I've written to my people. I have never found pause in preaching to them, but to read my own writings. I am afraid."

"I could read the rest of what you've written," I offered.

"I would like that. My scribe made two copies. One I have sent to Ephesus ahead of me. I have the other copy, so if you plan to join me upon the ship next week, perhaps the sea will brighten your mood and your suggestions will ease my doubts."

I envisioned myself hunched over a parchment to keep the spray of the water off it, bouncing up and down upon the waves. I grinned and felt a laugh nearly burst from within.

"We really haven't spoken much since we left my old vineyard," I said.

"No, and I am sorry," John said. He took my hand in his and squeezed it for a moment. "I have seen here again the hunger for any word about Christ. I need more than ever to know what you can tell me."

"First," I said, "please tell me. I heard you say when we looked at the burning Temple that Jesus foretold this destruction. How? And what else did he tell you?"

"Father Nicodemus," John said, suddenly with an air of deep seriousness. "I know the most important and dreadful thing that happened that night was the death of your Anna. I still grieve for her, and for all who were lost. So, please forgive me if this sounds cold. But, I don't really know how to explain it. So many thoughts came back to me that night. Thoughts about the things he had said to us. Everything he did."

I leaned closer to John. My heart pounded in my chest. I suddenly understood what I was desperate for. Something, anything, that would make sense of what happened to Anna and the others. Anything that could show God in control despite the Temple's destruction. Anything that could promise to one day lead us to our revenge against the soldiers who destroyed my family and home.

"We came to Jerusalem to prepare Passover dinner," John said.

I almost shouted at him. Passover dinner? I wanted to know God was still our God, that he had a plan for what had happened under the swords of the Romans. Was there a purpose for Anna's death? And now John was going to tell me about dinner?

"A few days earlier," John continued unaware, "Peter said what many of us secretly believed, that Jesus was the Messiah. James and I certainly believed it, we would go off into the hills alone and practice our swordsmanship with branches, getting ready for Jesus to lead us to victory. Well, Peter tells Jesus not to go to Jerusalem for Passover. He knew, I think, being older and wiser than the rest of us, what was going to happen. That Jesus was going to die. And Jesus scolded him harshly."

"What did he say?"

John stared at the fire and continued his story,

"So, when we came to the Passover, many of us were arguing over who was going to be first in the new kingdom. When Jesus walked into the room, we fell silent. I could see from his expression that he knew what we were discussing. Peter had been waiting next to where Jesus would sit. Even though he was our leader, his place at dinner never seemed important to him, until now. We were just simple fishermen, most of us. Tonight, though, after Jesus' rebuke, I suppose Peter felt the need to reconfirm his place."

John sighed deeply and stood. He looked down at the fire for some time, then held his hands out to his sides.

"Jesus said, 'the last shall be first'. And then he took me, the youngest and the least, and brought me to sit at his right hand. At his final Passover, he had me, of all people, sit by his side. And when Jesus then stripped down to slave's clothing and washed our feet one by one, Peter knew he had been singled out. He was being shown that he needed to be the servant to all, and yet he had come to this meal determined to be first. He even asked Jesus to wash all of him and not only his feet, he was so ashamed."

"That must have been a strange meal indeed," I whispered.

John half turned to me, his face dark in shadow.

"I don't know if Peter would have forsaken Jesus later that night if he hadn't been embarrassed before the rest of us as he had been. I don't know if I would have the courage to stand by Mary's side at the foot of the Cross had I not been chosen for that seat of honor. And yet, Jesus knew. He knew exactly what each of us needed. Then, when Jesus came back and told Peter that he was to serve everyone else, that he was to feed the sheep, that he was to lead us even to his own death, Peter was ready. And we were ready to receive him as our leader as well."

"And as for you?" I asked.

John shook his head.

"My fate? That the youngest would be the last survivor, I suppose. The most unlearned would become the teacher to many."

"And now, Rabbi," he said. "What of that night? What of your times with Jesus? Perhaps your story, the last to be told, will be among the first learned and loved by those who come after us."

I listened to the fire pop, watched it sparkle. The white foam of the waves reflected the gold and red of the fire. There seemed to be nothing of the world except for the two of us. How could the two of us possibly have been drawn together? In this place? At this time? Speaking of these issues?

For the first time, I felt as if the workings of God were in fact moving me, and us, toward this specific moment. Perhaps God had a purpose for all that had befallen my family and my people.

"John," I said. "I have only felt one thing. The day I met the young boy at the Temple. The day I heard Jesus preach on that hill. The night I spoke to him and he told me that the Spirit moves like the wind and goes not only where we plan."

I found myself suddenly unable to sit. I stood shakily, my old toes sinking in the hard sand, and moved to John's side. We stared at the flames together, warming our faces.

"I felt, here is the person who has the answers. More than that, here is a person who knew the questions. The right questions. I asked him about an earthly kingdom for our people. He understood that I did not really want or need that. That our people do not really need that. He asked me if I understood what I really needed. The Kingdom of Heaven, he meant. And then he asked me if I really understood the Spirit of God. It is there I have always been stuck. John, I still do not know what the right questions are. But, I believe you do. What are they, John? What are those questions?"

John sighed. He tilted his head back and stared into the black night above.

"Who is Jesus?" he said. "The question I always need to answer. Who is this man who came back from the dead and loved us beyond even how a mother loves her child? Who is this man who loved each of us as if we were his very own children? Children he wants to mature and become adults."

John turned toward me. He smiled broadly and my heart beat hard again in my chest.

"And how are we to follow him and treat each other as these adults? How are we to serve one another as he served us?"

We fell into silence. The cool night air brought with it a peace I had not enjoyed for a very long time. But a thought kept circling back to my lips until I could stand it no longer.

"How then do we serve him, and one another?" I asked. "How will the Spirit come to me? He said that it goes where it wills. Will it ever come to me, John? Please tell me."

John placed his hand upon my shoulder.

"Seek," he said, "and you will find. The door will be opened. Come with me and you might find what you desire."

Two weeks later, John told the believers in Antioch they were in good hands being led by a young leader named Ignatius who had learned about Christ from another named Barnabas. Barnabas had been known to us in Jerusalem, and had been a friend, according to the rumors we heard, of Saul. John told the others he must return to his own community in Ephesus.

The people gathered funds needed not only for John to sail to his destination, but for Miriam, Abram and myself as well. When we reached the docks, the two youngsters pointed me toward a small marker by the water. It designated the spot John's people said Saul first left the city to journey with the stories of Jesus to the Greeks and Jews in other great cities.

When we turned from the marker, the three of us stopped still, shocked. Despite the fact I was not only a Jew but a member of the Sanhedrin that had condemned their Lord, hundreds of John's people had come to send us on our way. They brought baskets of food, clothing and even a few coins to help us along. Most importantly, they treated me and my daughter with respect and friendship.

As we rolled up and down on the growing waves while exiting the bay of Antioch, I spoke with John.

"You risked a great deal seeking me out in Jerusalem," I said. "I want to thank you for continuing to care for us, for all you have done for me and my family. Especially when the Romans came."

"Rabbi," John said, "it is I who am thankful to you."

"How so?"

"I came to you, as the only other living eye-witness, and you gave me what I sought."

"The stories about Jesus?"

John shook his head. "No, not just the stories. But the image of who he was in life. It was a memory I had started to lose."

"But," I said, "you still seemed troubled."

John nodded.

"Nicodemus," he said, "in your words, I regained my friend Jesus as he was in life. I don't mean to anger you or bring back the painful memories of Anna. But I have to tell you, in the events of the Temple, and during our flight from Jerusalem, I have gained a new knowledge of Jesus."

"How so?"

John took a deep breath and sighed. "You brought back to me Jesus my friend and savior. The one I go to for the forgiveness of my sins. But the destruction of the Temple brought back to me Christ my Lord. I don't yet know how to explain it. But I can now again see him clearly as he was. After he brought himself back from the dead and walked among us again. Perhaps that is what I am meant to write."

Chapter 23

Ephesus

John took us from Antioch by boat, going first to Rhodes to shelter from the worst of the early spring squalls. From there we sailed on to our current home in Ephesus, landing just a month ago. My old body was devastated by the long journey, the never-ending roll of the waves, the baking sun. The crusty salt. So bad, it scratched my eyes every time I blinked.

After I slowly recovered, several Jews have now come to Ephesus, hearing perhaps that I was there. Some of the family names I knew. They are poor wanderers, each desperate to discover first-hand the fate of our City and our Temple. Like lost sheep, they want to go back to Jerusalem for Passover, and yet we have all by now heard that there is no Temple to return to. Nothing but the smell of the soot and ash I still taste when I breath deep.

John joined us the previous evening and after our last group of visitors left, he remained with me. He was now grim. One of the visiting Jews had lived in the Upper City when the Romans attacked. He followed the southern road away from the Temple. John covered his eyes as the man told of the Roman legion marching along that road the day following our flight from the vineyard. They continued their destruction for miles, all along the route John's people travelled in the weeks preceding the attack. After our guests left, I tried to console my young friend. Instead, he sighed deeply, nodded and turned consoled my bitter thoughts.

"All these years," he said, "I led my people and I still never understood."

He told me some of Jesus' teachings. He told of how Jesus once spoke to a Samaritan woman, of all people, far away from the crowds. He had told her, "Woman, believe me, an hour is coming when neither in this mountain nor in Jerusalem will you worship the Father."

Perhaps, I thought blackly. Perhaps.

I was there when Jesus predicted the destruction of the Temple. I heard his words myself, at his trial. But, was John now saying that through this chaos and death, John had come to believe in Jesus in a different way?

The following morning, and I sat on the edge of my bed and looked at the outline of a fish scratched into the inside of my door.

"God in heaven," I said, "if you knew the Romans would come, did you now also know Anna would be butchered? Did she have to die? Was this part of your plan? Why?"

I shook the thoughts from my mind with an effort. I closed my eyes and focused my thoughts.

"I offer thanks to you," I prayed, "living and eternal King, for you have mercifully restored my soul within me; Your faithfulness is great."

I looked to the ceiling and opened my arms out to my sides,

"Bless the Lord, O my soul, and all that is within me, bless his holy name!"

All remained quiet. Off in the distance, I heard a cock crow. Nearby, there were the grunts and snorts of various farm animals. The daily business of Ephesus had not yet begun. It was Sunday. There were many Christ-followers in this city now, and none of them would work this day. For, in fact, this wasn't only an ordinary Sunday.

This day was for them the most holy of days. The day John and his people celebrate their risen Christ. Their pascha.

All week, there had been remembrances. Some happy, some sorrowful. John had stood before his people two nights ago and recalled the last time he and his fellows supped with their Lord. As he spoke, I noticed several scribes in the gathering writing down his words. It seemed, perhaps, that John need not have come to me to help write his recollections the previous year, there were plenty of others eager to help him.

For the first time, I had stayed among them for their meal. John had told me, first upon our trek from Jerusalem to Ephesus and several times since, how Jesus had called himself the true bread from heaven. He told me, I think, so I might provide for him further support from the Torah concerning Jesus' words, how Jesus had established a new covenant the night before he was crucified. I often think of that day. How my Sanhedrin plotted his death even as he held one last meal with his friends.

But it wasn't until John's description of that meal to the believers here in Ephesus that it finally became real to me. At their gathering the eve of the Sabbath, John told stories about the last night Jesus lived in the world, and the day of his death. I could now picture this Jesus, who I had twice betrayed, soon to hang above me on a cross, enjoying a moment of friendship with those he loved. Did he know then? He had made his way into the Holy City in a very public way. Had he known even as he held up a piece of bread and blessed his friends what was about to befall him?

I shook my head, forcing these recent memories from my mind. I realized I was now simply looking up only at my ceiling. Still utterly alone.

Slowly, I brought my hands together before my lap. I rolled to my right and let my weight slide me off the edge of my bed. My knees hit the floor and I wobbled for a moment. I held myself still and I closed my eyes. I saw the face of Jesus, reflecting the firelight as I recalled our one evening talk so long ago. He smiled at me then, and now. Inviting me to be born of the spirit. His spirit. God's spirit. He teased me, challenging me as to why I, an educated leader of the Chosen People, could not understand.

"Help me to understand," I now whispered. "Help me, Jesus."

This time my legs buckled, and I slid along the edge of the bed and I crashed to the floor. I covered my face with trembling hands. I felt him standing before me. Reaching his hand out to me. Inviting me to love him as he seemed to love me. Despite my betrayals. Despite my unwillingness to believe all these years.

Two hours later, as the sun rose over Ephesus on this, their resurrection day, John stood before his large congregation. His people. His church. He silently looked at the bread and wine before him.

He paused, then looked at me with a smile.

"Many of you have seen my friend with me these past weeks," he said.

I gasped. Brood ran from my face. My head and hands shook.

John smiled ever more broadly. Someone in the congregation leaned close from behind, and a hand was gently laid upon my shoulder. A woman seated just to my right looked at me and reached out to squeeze my hand.

"My friend's name is Nicodemus," John said. "He is not one of us, he is a son of Abraham from the Temple. He was once a member of the Sanhedrin. He lost his own daughter there that terrible night last year."

There was a murmur among the people around me. The woman to my side let go of my hand. But the hand on my shoulder tightened slightly in reassurance. My eyes locked upon John.

John lifted his hand out to me. "My friend," he said. "You are the last person alive, other than me, who saw Jesus in the flesh."

John swept his arm left to right above the gathering.

"This man," he said loudly, "defended our Lord on the night of his condemnation. This man stood at the foot our Lord's Cross as he died. This man buried our Lord the evening of his death. This man has shown me again the Jesus I knew once again."

One by one the others stood and turned toward me.

"Rabbi?" John said, motioning for me to join him before the rest.

I tried to stand, unsteadily. I gripped the hand that had reassured me from behind for support. I turned to look at who was helping me stand. There, just behind me, stood a Roman soldier, bare headed, tears running down his face. He opened his mouth to say something. His lower lip quivered, and he dropped his eyes to the floor.

I stepped back from the man, horrified. But as I turned, I witnessed nothing but smiles, bright faces eager in anticipation. The people moved to either side, and John stepped off to platform to receive me.

He helped me onto the low platform, and we turned to the people.

"Rabbi Nicodemus," he said. "Could you please tell us something about the Lord we are about to receive?"

My mouth was dry. I voice squeaked in my ears.

"I am not one of you," I said. "And I am no hero."

John placed his warm hand upon my back. My eyes were drawn to the Roman who had stood behind me. He sat now, hands covering his face. I glanced up to the ceiling.

"I tried to pray this morning," I said. "And all I thought about was the face of your Jesus. He was once in my arms, cold and limp. His face and body were cut and bruised, and here, in his side, a spear had plunged in deep. But that is not the Jesus I saw this morning."

I looked down at the people. Many stood now, hand in hand. A few of the women fought back tears.

"The face I saw was the face that looked at me one beautiful sunny day. I stood maybe thirty paces from him. And I had just watched as he walked right up to a leper, touched the man's scarred face and then...and then the leper was clean. Jesus looked at me and, in that moment, I knew that I, as a priest, was now called to receive this leper, this outcast."

I paused and shuddered. My eyes were drawn again to the Roman. As I gathered myself, he noticed my silence and looked up. Our eyes met and he slowly nodded.

"But I could not. I ran off, ran off from my duty. Ignored his call for me to love this leper. Ignored my responsibility to reach out to those who are outcast."

I paused again. My neck felt thick. John came close and asked quietly if I was alright. I nodded and forced myself to go on.

"Your Jesus asked the right questions. He can help you ask the right questions. He asked me one day, and it has now taken me almost forty years to allow myself to accept it, 'are you ready to allow the God of the Chosen People to now be God to all?' I thought, if he is God to all, how am I to treat those who are not of my own people?"

I tried to look back at the Roman, but could not. I only wanted to slink away, to hide behind John and out of sight. I felt a shame so deep as to rip away any good I may ever had done. I reached up to my head to rip off my Pharisaic covering, only to remember I had left it far behind in Jerusalem. I turned away from John's touch and sat far to the edge of the platform.

John waited. He then said with a rough voice, "May we pray for you, brother Nicodemus. May your experience with Jesus be our experience."

"And," he continued as he moved again to the table with the bread and wine, "may we continue to experience him now in the most special way."

"He loved me," John said, more to himself than to all of us.

"He loved me," he said again, loudly. "I leaned against him during that last supper. We sat together, we laughed together. He walked with us, both before and after his Resurrection."

He looked at the people gathered before him.

"And he loves you. I am the last of the Twelve. I am the only one in this room, except for our friend Nicodemus, who ever saw or heard the Lord in person."

He paused and waited until I looked up at him.

"He loves all of you as he loved me. And he," he said, motioning to the loaves, "promised to be with you as he was with me. With you, he also wants to touch, to embrace, to unite."

He paused. He blinked slowly, then looked again at me. He looked for so long that those before me begin to stir. John then looked to the heavens and a smile came over his face. He looked again to me and mouthed the words, *I know.*

I know? I thought. My heart thumped in my chest. I was so excited I found I could not breathe. My young friend, perhaps now my teacher, finally understood what he had been called to write about his Lord. He found his purpose.

Blood rushed to my face. My hands tingled. I felt overwhelmingly compelled to stand. I forced myself to my feet, slowly unfolding my stiff back and neck.

"I have been asked by many of you," John said, "to write about our Lord. I feel entirely unworthy of the task. But, I will begin to tell you now the story...."

John raised his hands, closed his eyes and bowed his head.

When he spoke then, his deep voice rumbled through the gathering and echoed off the walls.

"In the beginning," he said.

Some near me took the hands of those around them. I noticed for the first time then, men holding hands with their women. Parents with their children. The Roman still in uniform, a tradesman from the far east dressed as those who once searched for an infant King. A man tattooed as if from Africa, a nobleman from Egypt. Some in the fine silk of Antioch, others in rags.

John waited and those in the congregation edged closer to where he stood and fell utterly silent.

"In the beginning," he repeated, motioning again to the table before him, "was the Word."

He opened his eyes and glanced once more in my direction, though I doubt he could see me among the throng standing around me. I opened my mouth and gasped before his intense eyes.

"In the beginning was the Word. And the Word was with God."

John paused and a great smile, the great smile of both joy and relief, spread across his face.

"And the Word was God!"

He slowly walked around the table and stepped into the crowd. He reached out with both hands and cupped the faces of the nearest people with open palms. He smiled at them and moved on to another two, and then another.

"And our Father loves us. Loves us, all of us, and sent his Word to us. He sent his Word so that anyone who believes in this Word shall have eternal life. That everyone who believes in Jesus the Christ will be saved and will have life to its fullest."

John circled back to the platform. He looked down, mouthing words in silence. He moved his fingers slightly in front of him, almost as if he was writing. I realized he finally knew what he was to write.

He looked up after a few moments. There was not a sound about me. The people stared at their leader in a combination of joy and wonder. Many also had their eyes closed, especially those like me who still wore the garments of our Jewish forefathers.

John moved his head slowly left, then right. He held his hands out to his sides, palms up to the heavens.

Then he looked directly at me, his dark eyes wide and intent.

"I have now told you who my friend Jesus was. I have told you what my Lord, the Christ, is. We are here today to celebrate that morning, thirty-eight years ago, when we found his tomb empty. The day he walked back through our locked door and granted us his peace."

"But I want to share once more what happened that Friday upon that dreadful hill. My friend hung upon a cross. And he looked down at me, at his mother, at the Jewish leaders. He looked down at the Romans crucifying him. And he cried out to the father. He cried out - 'Father forgive them!' He cried out - 'They do not know what they do!'"

"In this moment of agony, my friend forgave those who rejected and murdered him. He forgave Jew and Gentile alike. For he knew even then that he would give us, all of us, his Spirit. As he once said, 'The Spirit is like the wind and goes where it wills'. The Spirit of God is not constrained by whether we were once Gentile or Jew, he reaches out for all of us, for we are all his children. We have all sinned through our pride, through our ignorance, the passions and lusts of our bodies. We are all sinners in equal need of salvation through Christ. If we believe. If we forgive. If we follow and obey."

The people then repeated the prayer taught to John by Jesus himself. I had heard the words often enough this past year but for the first time I contemplated a loving father reaching out to his children. I thought of what I myself needed forgiveness for, and wondered, can I have this blessing only 'as' I gave it to others?

A long dormant and unrecognizable hope sprang within me. My mind battled fiercely, throwing before me all my guilt and failures. I saw again the babies - the babies! - dead in their mothers' arms so long ago. And Anna, letting her go to be butchered at the very wall of the Temple. Tears bit my eyes. My body shook and shook.

When the people recited the words given by their Lord to forgive those who had hurt them....

When I myself muttered, 'as I forgive those who had sinned against me," my legs gave way and I collapsed heavily to my knees.

My head hung forward. I trembled deep in my chest. A few hands touched me, not trying to pull me up as much as simply being with me. I muttered, 'no, no.'

They finished their prayer.

"We were terrified of Jesus then," John then said, "this day all those years ago. We had failed him. Deserted him. But he came back to us nonetheless and instead of wrath he gave us his peace. Please give this same peace to those around you now."

More hands touched me now. I few faces came close. Then I felt those next to me pull back and another person stepped close.

A face came near mine and I could smell my granddaughter even before I heard Miriam's voice.

"Peace, grandfather."

Miriam leaned close and her lips kissed me warmly on my temple. Her tears mixed with my own trickling down my cheek. I reached for her and she pulled me up. We stood for a long moment, holding each other tight.

She kissed me again and turned back toward Abram. His eyes were reddened as he looked back at John. I wiped the tears from my eyes and also looked toward the platform. John clasped his hands together and began to walk off the platform directly toward me!

I panicked. How could I face a man like this? The holiness. The holiness! The Lord had spoken through him this very day!

I turned and bounced off a large man standing to my left. I pushed past him and rushed toward the door. I heard Miriam's sweet voice calling after me. But I had to find the light of day. I could not breathe.

Chapter 24

The Wind

I fled John's assembly an hour ago. I grabbed the first walking stick I found leaning against the doorway and stumbled through the streets of Ephesus. Miriam's kiss cooled upon my forehead when I left the gathering. Now, I am sweating heavily in the mid-spring sun.

To my right is the great theater, carved deep into the hillside. Rows of empty stone seats curve hundreds of feet away from me. I am halfway up that hillside now. I am surprised I have made it this far but the past hour has been but a blur. I thought I heard Miriam's voice call for me once or twice. But my thoughts and senses have been trapped, looking within.

What did I feel back there? When they prayed together to their abba?

Who stood next to me listening to John? Gentiles, women, a Roman soldier? All of them believing in this Jesus? Who was this man? How could he offer forgiveness to all these people? How could he possibly offer forgiveness to me for all I have done?

And yet what do I feel now? Hope? But why?

"Because the Word was with God, and the Word was God?"

As I repeat John's words, I expect to curse and deny them out of hand. But I can't. Was not Jesus the one I saw heal a leper? Was he not the one who just an hour ago brought me and Gentiles together in worship? Was he not the one I once betrayed as an infant, and the same man hung above me on that cross asking his father to forgive? To forgive? Even me?

Look there, to the right. Those broken statues and columns are all that remains from the great temple of Isis that once stood here.

Emperor Augustus destroyed this place, right around the time this Jesus was born. Right around the time I betrayed the infants of Bethlehem.

They destroyed this temple as they have now desolated the Holy Temple of Jerusalem. God above, what does that mean? This temple to Isis has not been rebuilt, the goddess it honored is no longer honored even here in her city. Are we to go follow this same path? Is this our fate?

This climb is getting more difficult. The top of the hill is within sight. Why do I feel so compelled to make it to the peak?

"No. Our people will not be forgotten. Maybe John is right. He said Jesus told them he was the Temple and that he would rise again. Maybe God is still at work through our pain and exile. Maybe his Temple has already been rebuilt."

But then who are the people of this new Temple? To whom has this Jesus brought the opportunity to belong? The women back there in town, the ones sitting near me in John's gathering? The Gentiles? The Gentiles! The...the Roman soldier who reached out and touched me? He murdered Anna just a year ago! Is he also called?

"The wind blows wherever it pleases. You hear its sound, but you cannot tell where it comes from or where it is going. So it is with everyone born of the Spirit."

Is that what you meant, Jesus? That those people down there all have the opportunity to believe? I came to you as a priest of the Chosen People and I demanded you to give yourself only to us. But is this what you meant? That the Spirit of God can also go to these other people if it chooses?

I stop. My legs shake beneath me. I look up and squint against the sun.

"Can you then also choose me? A sinner? Can you forgive me Lord of my treachery?"

Again, I cannot breathe. I lean against the walking stick, staring down into the dust. I don't know if I can make another step. My heart pounds. My breath roars hot in my throat. I must move on.

There! I have made the top of the hill. Below me, stretching as far as I can see, the deep blue of the sea. The white foam of the waves. The bright, sandy beach.

The wind.

I close my eyes. The breeze cools my hair and blows back my robes.

The wind.

The Spirit is like the wind.

I can't hold my head steady any longer. It is rolling back. I stare into the clear blue sky.

"Send your Spirit. Send your Spirit like the wind, Lord. Forgive me. Take me back."

The roll of the waves. The call of the gulls. The burning in my heart. The peace. The peace seeping into my mind.

"If you will it, Lord, be my Father."

THE END

About the Author

Rick Akins is a father of three and currently lives in Wheaton, Illinois, a suburb of Chicago. He was born and raised Catholic in upstate New York and has an electrical engineering degree and MBA from the University of Illinois.

Rick has been widely published in the technology field and owns six patents in fiber optics. In 2004, he began attending an evangelical church every other weekend for family reasons and wrote several books about the experience.

He is a member of St. Michael Catholic Parish and remains active in the field of ecumenism.